# T...
and ot... stories

# THE ICE
## and other stories

# Kenneth Steven

ARGYLL✠PUBLISHING

© Kenneth Steven 2010

First published in 2010 by
Argyll Publishing
Glendaruel
Argyll PA22 3AE
Scotland
www.argyllpublishing.com

The author has asserted his moral rights.

**British Library Cataloguing-in-Publication Data.**
**A catalogue record for this book is available from**
**the British Library.**

ISBN 978 1 906134 46 4

*Printing:* J F Print Ltd, Somerset

*This book is for my brother John*

# CONTENTS

Acknowledgements    9

The Ice    11

Conquering    47

Teddy Fry    55

Lemon Ice Cream    65

The Pearl    73

Billy    97

Cloudberries    107

The Sledge    113

The Gift    121

Kilninian    129

The Song of a Robin    135

Clockwork    143

A Christmas Child    151

The Typewriter    156

# ACKNOWLEDGEMENTS

Sections from 'The Ice' were dramatised by students from the Royal Scottish Academy of Music and Drama in Glasgow for a programme of mine on bullying produced and broadcast by BBC Radio Scotland. At the time of going to press 'The Ice' has been accepted for publication by the US literary journal *Relief*. It has been published in Scotland by the online magazine *The Caledonia Review*. 'The Pearl' was published by the literary journal *Markings*; it was then taken by the dramatist Keith Simpson and turned into an award-winning one act play. 'Billy' and 'Lemon Ice Cream' were broadcast by BBC Radio 4 as part of their afternoon short story series, as was a longer version of 'The Sledge'. This latter story and 'Cloudberries' were published by *The People's Friend*. 'Billy' was published in the Welsh literary journal *Planet*; 'The Sledge' and 'Kilninian' in *Leopard*. 'Conquering' appeared in the online magazine *The Glasgow Review*. 'Lemon Ice Cream' appeared in *New Writing Scotland* and will be published in an American anthology of Sicilian stories. 'Teddy Fry' was published in *The New Writer*; 'Applegarth' appeared in *The French Literary Review*. 'The Gift' was taken for the pages of *Ireland's Own* and published in Scotland in *Life and Work*, who also commissioned 'A Christmas Child'.

Finally, 'Billy', 'Herring', 'Lemon Ice Cream' and 'The Gift' are all on the Shortbread website, an online home dedicated to the furtherance of the short story.

Kenneth Steven
January 2010

# The Ice

**For the last three miles of the drive, once they were on the**
Hallion estate proper, Lewis felt as though he wasn't there.
Perhaps it was the motion of the car on the bumpy track, and
the warmth of the vehicle with its steamed-up windows. It
felt as though his hands and feet were melting away completely
and all he heard from far away was the hum of the engine.

Harry didn't say anything either. He'd asked the odd thing
when he met the boy at the station; quizzed him about bags
and boxes and what could go where in the boot. But somehow
he sensed there was no point asking more, about what
Glenellen was like and how the first term had passed. Lewis
sat there with his eyes fixed straight ahead, his crumpled coat
still held under his right arm, there and yet not there at all.

It was only when suddenly they came through the dark
forest of rhododendron and swung round to the left into a
wide bend that the boy seemed to come alive. There was a

glint of silver in the trees, through the birches, and he was wiping the misted window, making a hole to see.

'Woodpeckers this morning,' Harry said, filling the silence. 'Two of them down at the feeders behind the Lodge.'

But Lewis was looking away left, through the thinning trees to the grey expanse of water. He was there and yet he wasn't there, and when all of a sudden they bounded over a last bump and the tall white walls of the Lodge were finally visible, he unclipped the seatbelt and opened the door before Harry had properly stopped.

'Will you wait!' he exclaimed, but there was no point. The boy was running down between tree roots and rusted clumps of bracken towards the water. The engine fluttered and died. A scattering of mallard close to the shore took fright, scrabbled into the air, complaining. Harry sat there still, listening to the silence, watching the silhouette of the boy against the grey-white water, as the back door of the Lodge banged and a tall man in a tweed jacket started over the gravel towards the car. Harry got out in a hurry, began pulling out the boy's luggage.

'I'd like you to have a look at the fence above Croft Hill, Harry. The deer must be getting through again. Have you time?'

A violin in its dark case was the last thing to be brought out and put down upright onto the track.

'Yes, sir, I'll go once I've seen to the track. The water's made quite a mess of it. A real crater.'

Suddenly the man looked down towards the water. The boy was still there, small and dark against the pale surface of the lake. Far out, over towards the opposite shore, was an islet, crowded with tall trees and dark shadows of undergrowth.

The Ice and other stories

'And how's he?' asked the man, not looking round.

Harry paused, watching him.

'Seems fine. Very eager to get down to the water!'

They both laughed and Harry began carting in the bags. The man kept where he was and took out a cigarette; the blue smoke of it hung in the still air as he stood there. When the first bags went into the hall he heard a muffled voice from upstairs; Harry's name was all he made out. Then his mother was there, looking round anxiously in all directions.

'Lewis!' she shouted. 'Where are you, Lewis?'

It was so still her voice carried, echoed even over the water into the hill on the far shore. The boy turned and seemed to run even as he did so; it was as though there was no gap between his turning and his running. He flew up through the bracken in one sure line towards that voice.

The cigarette's thin blue coil drifted into the still air.

'Mind your coat, Lewis!'

He watched the boy as he ran, his eyes dark, but the boy didn't look at him. It was as though he hadn't heard. He poured himself straight into the arms of the elderly woman in her wide white skirts and checked jacket. She buried her hands in his hair.

•

He stayed in the couch in her sitting room until the clock in the hall fluttered seven times. He lay curled on the couch, his face turned away and buried in the cushion, as if fast asleep. She sat beside him a long time, her hand in the straight dark gold of his hair. He talked to her after he had stopped crying;

he talked to her in angry fragments about the Latin teacher, about Saturday nights after prep, about the way the nurse had treated him after he fell on the stairs. But most of all he talked about swimming, about the stone cold place where they waited for the games master, and all that happened before he came. She felt herself there too with those thin, white boys as the shouting echoed around the walls and the voice shook those who couldn't swim and dug into their helplessness. Her fingers ran over the soft skin at the nape of his neck and she felt, in spite of herself, a welling at the back of her own eyes. But she fought it away and brushed her hand fiercely over her eyes and he didn't notice; she was glad he didn't notice. . .

'Lewis, it's almost time for dinner. You haven't unpacked a thing and I haven't written my letter. Come on, your father hasn't seen you either!'

She moved but he didn't. She looked back at him, curled there on the couch, and suddenly she remembered him two years before, in the weeks after Kate had died. This was where he had come and this was how he had lain – just the same, only a little smaller. And she heard the memory of that crying she could never forget; the long, slow ocean of it, exhausted and broken, like some terrible song. He had talked to her too then, and that was how he felt safest – turned away, his head buried in the pillow and his eyes closed, her hand at the back of his hair. She had given him then a little white elephant her husband had once carved. He was dying when he made it for her; he didn't say so but she knew it was to be a way of remembering him. Now it was for Lewis and no-one else, to hold when he was so low he could take no more. It was to be something to take back with him to Glenellen, to carry always in his pocket. She remembered that and she sat down again beside him, her hand suddenly even gentler than before. He noticed and half-turned, not understanding. His face was glassy and broken.

'Listen,' she said, taking hold of his hand instead. 'I have an idea. The island on the lake.'

Now he had sat up, was watching her.

'Your grandfather had a house out there, you know. It wasn't much more than a cabin, but when he was a child he called it the Christmas House. One winter he stayed there, when there was enough ice on the lake. It was something he never forgot. Why don't you go there this Christmas, with your brother and your cousin Winifred, if the ice is strong enough?'

'To stay out there?' Lewis asked, not blinking. 'Would we be able to stay out there?'

She nodded, almost regretting what she'd said, as her son called from downstairs that dinner was ready, that it had been for twenty minutes.

•

Roddy came home the following Friday. Even though he was only fourteen he had persuaded Harry to let him drive up the track once they were off the main road. His father was out checking pheasant pens and met them on the track a quarter of a mile from the Lodge; he all but strung Roddy up by the thumbs from the nearest birch tree, his face pulped to a purple fury. He didn't speak to Harry for the next two days, just left the sparsest scraps of notes for him in the porch.

Lewis felt confused when he saw his brother from the landing window. His heart thudded and he felt there were things to hide away. He felt confused and frightened, and the fact that he was frightened made him confused. But they laughed together about Roddy being caught on the track, and that was all right. He wanted to tell Roddy about the Christmas House, but he wasn't sure, his mouth closed again.

'What was it like?' he asked instead.

Roddy looked up from his bags. 'The corps training? Awful, as bad as it could have been. Fuzzy was in charge of my group. At least Macgregor wasn't there, though.'

Lewis felt his cheeks sting with warmth. Macgregor took him for swimming. He was the worst of the lot, week after relentless week. Suddenly he smelled Glenellen again in the stale clothes that Roddy spilled out over the floor. He smelled school and wanted it gone, he wanted it to have no place here; he didn't want it to spoil what was precious. . .

That afternoon he went running up Croft Hill in the last of the light. He didn't stop until he'd got to the top, seven hundred feet up, and when he did he stood there panting, his palms on his knees. His father said you could see the whole estate, every corner of it, from the summit. All that mattered to Lewis was to see the lake; this was the best place, from here he had an eagle's eye view. He dug out his grandfather's precious monocular from its chestnut case, crouched in the long grass and forced his breathing to slow.

The magnified circle crossed the lake and found the islet. There was a beach on the near side, the one facing him. He followed what might have been a path further in, through

The Ice and other stories

birches and bushes to something round, something made of wood. He heard his heart. There was a window in the near side, small and thin, like the kind of window in a medieval castle or church. It wasn't quite in the middle, the house; the very heart of the islet looked a tangle of trees and brambles. He circled the whole of it, saw at the very far end a line of stones, and there on the last of them a heron, hunched in his grey overcoat. It looked as though there had been a place for a fire there; he was sure he could see a rough ring of stones. All at once he imagined them out there long years ago, not in the middle of winter at all but at midsummer. The night was blue and the orange glow of a fire lit their faces; laughter echoed over the water and someone was daring to swim. They had pulled off all their clothes and crashed into the water at the south end of the island; they were splashing and laughing and the rest of them were watching, applauding.

•

That night Lewis was back at Glenellen. He was there in the wandered tangle of his dreams that was dense as the island's jungle heart. He was back in the first week, on the first day of swimming. He could hear the drip of water as they waited, twenty-four white figures with their feet together, toes touching the pool edge. It was like the drip of time itself.

A prefect was there in his uniform. Mr Macgregor would be over in a few minutes; this was a chance to talk about a swimming gala to be held in October. It was an inter-house gala; they all knew by now the importance of representing their houses, didn't they? Twenty-four heads nodded and the drip ticked, ticked. The boy's black shoes echoed dully on the cold stone as he paced up and down at the deep end. How many of them would still be twelve on the thirteenth of October? A flutter of hands. How many of them were thirteen now?

Lewis was confused. He kept his hand in the air after the others had fallen, and the prefect noticed. The shoes stopped. His question echoed in the stone.

'Please, sir, it's my birthday today. What should I do?'

A slow smile spread over the prefect's face. It was like a flame creeping across paper after lit by a match.

'What should you do? Well, to begin with, you shouldn't call me sir.' There was a slow snigger from twenty-three figures; now they were watching and enjoying. 'Secondly, you should come up here.'

Lewis was almost right down at the shallow end. He moved as though through water, his bare feet treading the shimmer of thin pools on the surface of the stone. He didn't understand. He was freezing cold.

The prefect was grinning. He had bad breath.

'What's your name?'

'Lewis. I mean Cameron.'

'Right, Cameron, happy birthday!'

The prefect lifted him as if he had been no more than a bit of balsa wood, carried him up to the top diving board, and tipped him out into the deep end. Lewis came to the surface, swallowing and choking, swirling his arms to reach the side, the laughter and applause sore in his ears. He couldn't swim.

•

That Sunday there was a party at the Lodge. The skies had cleared; the rain of the last ten days was over and the skies turned a luminous blue. There wasn't a whisper of sound by the lake. Lewis cracked a twig underfoot, and the echo of it seemed to carry right through the bowl of the hills like a gunshot. It was going to freeze that night; it would be the first night of frost. He turned back and looked over at the islet; it was nothing more than a dark shadow hunched on the surface of the water, its taller trees searching like the fingers of twisted hands into the sky. This was going to be the first night of frost. His heart sang.

The boys ate at five at a table set for them by their grandmother in front of a dragon of red fire. By the time Lewis was halfway through his plate of venison and potatoes his shins were tartan with the heat of it.

'Why can't we come to the party?' Roddy asked through a last mouthful of venison.

'Because you can't,' his father said, looking out of the side window onto the track, a cigarette held in his right hand. He didn't look round.

The cars came in soft curves up the track, their headlights turning the hillsides vivid gold. Voices and laughter were warm in the yard; plumes of white breath clouded the night, the night that had left diamonds on sills and roofs. Lewis watched from the window of their bedroom and all at once he missed his mother so badly it was sore as a rusty knife in his stomach. He felt the edge of the elephant in his pocket; he dug it into his forefinger. He yearned for her. Whenever he remembered she filled him like a gust of longing and he was blown out of himself. Nothing in all the world mattered then, nothing but that longing.

The cars shone in the yard under a cold ball of moon like a single eye. Everyone had arrived now; the rooms downstairs sounded strange with their river of loud talk and laughter, the clink of cutlery and glasses.

Roddy came over to the window and opened it.

'Look,' he hissed, and brought out a miniature bottle of whisky and a cigarette.

'Got them from dad.' That was in answer to the loud questions in Lewis's white face.

Lewis didn't enjoy either, though he pretended to. He was too terrified of the apparition of his grandmother at the door, and of the consequences. He felt dizzy after the cigarette and sick after the whisky.

He ate mints and brushed his teeth twice, scrubbed at his face as though scraping moss from stone, and gargled. Then he lay in bed long after Roddy's breath had grown soft and easy, until the car doors began to thud and the *good nights* were loud in the darkness, until the last voices had gone from the hall. He padded out onto the landing and looked for his grandmother. He sat there ten minutes, crouching and shivering. At last she appeared, wheezing, her hand slow on the banister, and turned to go up her own stair.

'How thick does the ice need to be, granny?' he hissed.

She looked round, paused, not understanding for a second. Then her eyes lit up and she smiled.

'Three and a half inches,' she said.

•

John Cameron was up before it was light the following day. He hadn't slept well; he had what his own father would have called a whisky head. He went out into the dark blue stillness of the morning, his coat buttoned against the first frost of winter. It must have been five below during the night. He heard something through the trees at the back of the Lodge, under Croft Hill. Ragged voices, the flight of half a dozen greylag geese. He heard them but couldn't see them. He remembered the last goose he had shot the year before, over on the far shore of the lake. He had found it, still flapping and broken, its long neck stretched on the shore. It was trying so hard, flailing, and in that second he thought of Kate, two days before she died in the white lie of that city hospital. He looked back at the goose and something in him broke too.

He went down to the lake that morning. The bracken bristled with frost; sharp panes of ice crackled underfoot as he walked. It was beginning to grow grey; he saw the edge of the water as he came close. Except that it wasn't water, it was a white skin of ice. He put out one foot and heard the crack of it as it broke; it was thicker than he had imagined, though a few feet out the deeper water remained black and clear. They had said it would be a long winter, and a cold one – perhaps Lewis would get his wish. An edge of smile twisted his mouth. His mother should never have put such a hope into his head all the same; how many nights of frost would it take to bring that kind of ice? They'd made the lake a hundred years and more ago for curling; back then it could be frozen for weeks through the winter, and the village well-nigh deserted for the match.

The cabin on the island had been built by his great grand-father for those curling matches. A place to serve hot toddy and spiced wine; a place to have a glowing brazier on days when the hands turned to raw, red, useless stumps. It was his father who'd called it the Christmas House, and several winters on the trot he'd gone out there as a boy to stay, taking everything he needed with him over the ice.

But how long since they'd had winters like that? John Cameron picked up a shard of the ice he'd broken and turned it in his left hand. Perhaps this was all they'd get. He skimmed it away and stood up, suddenly cold himself. The hills were beginning to appear out of the darkness. Up beside the Lodge he heard the soft riches of a blackbird's song; it was so beautiful he had to pause there on the track, cold or no cold. And he remembered another blackbird, however many years before, that had sung in the back courts of the city when he was a student there. It had sung out of the darkness and he had made up his mind that when he was done with his studies he would go back to Hallion after all, that he had to.

•

'Why is Winifred coming for Christmas?' Roddy asked at breakfast. 'Don't they celebrate Christmas in Manchester?'

His father folded his paper and looked at him as a woodpecker might contemplate a nut. But he had no answer.

Their grandmother lifted the teapot to top it up with hot water.

'Winifred is coming because her parents are going to the Lake District. They decided that for a treat she should come north to us, which is why it's up to you two to make sure her time here is special.'

Lewis hadn't seen his cousin since his mother died. She had been there at the church and had shaken his hand on the way out. He remembered her eyes, her very brown eyes – that was the only thing. She hadn't said anything but she'd just looked right at him, as if she was saying something after all.

'That's not the reason Winifred's coming here,' Roddy said upstairs, thumping down onto his bed and yawning. 'I heard gran talking to her parents ages ago; they're probably getting a divorce. I reckon they're going away on their own to get peace and quiet. Sort the whole thing out.'

Lewis thought about that, and about Winifred's brown eyes, when he went up to the attic. He'd done his chore for the day, but he had to wait in the house until Winifred arrived at lunch-time.

The skylight window was covered with crystals of frost. He went over to stare up at it, that patterning of thousands of gems. He couldn't see the sky through it, that was how thick the frost was.

He started rummaging through one of the old boxes on the floor, a collection of Cameron things that had found their way there from castles and terraced houses and old boats. There was a rubber ball that he bounced against the wall until it leapt over his head and started bounding downstairs. He couldn't be bothered going after it. There were some of his father's rugby shirts from Glenellen; there was his name in Gothic script along the inside of the collar. He felt funny holding those.

Then he pulled out a black radio. He was always fascinated by radios; you could twist a dial and hear voices from all over the world in different languages. Sometimes they were far away, as if they were trying to speak through a storm of crackling, and suddenly so clear it was as though they were there in the same room. The thing was bound to be dead; the batteries would have given out years before.

He clicked the dial all the same and bent down to listen. It wasn't even a crackling, just a very far off hiss. For some reason he thought it was like mist, but that wasn't a sound. He turned the dial very slowly; sometimes the mist lessened, and perhaps there was the ghost of a voice at the back of it. He kept on; bent right over with his ear hard against the radio, hoping.

Then suddenly a voice. A woman's clear English; every word enunciated:

'. . . for England and Wales it will be much the same story. About five or six in sheltered inland districts, but several degrees warmer elsewhere, especially along the south coast. In Scotland the weather's set to get much colder as high pressure moves in from Scandinavia; tonight we could be looking at a dip to minus ten. . .'

Lewis clicked off the radio. He crouched there still, a beautiful warmth flooding his heart.

•

'Train was an hour and a half late. Heavy snow in the Lake District.'

Harry staggered into the hall with a case, several odd-shaped parcels and a very thinly disguised whisky bottle which John Cameron helped to safety.

'Winifred, you must be exhausted! Come in, dear, and welcome to the Lodge. You remember Roddy, and Lewis would have been a couple of inches smaller when you last saw him.'

The brown eyes were exactly as he remembered them. She was like a parcel herself, wrapped up in Manchester against the legendary cold of Scotland. Granny Cameron wound away layer after layer as Winifred smiled and watched; and the boys stood there like wounded caribou, not knowing what to do.

'Come on, then! Show your cousin some courtesy! Off up to the study and get warm, Winifred, and make sure these two look after you. In fact, take Winifred to her room first, Roddy, and just come down when you're ready. We'll restore you with tea and cake!'

Later on, as it was getting dark, Lewis asked if she'd like to go down to see the lake. The brown eyes nodded. His heart thumped, but he felt all right, and he had to tell her. Outside, the stars were firing in sharp white gems above their heads. They had to stop in the fierce blue cold.

'You can't really see the stars in Manchester,' she said.

'Not like that.'

Her head was turned right up to look; in the light of the porch lamp he could see the gold hair that curled about her eyes.

'Come on,' he said. 'You have to see the lake!'

He almost felt as though he had made it himself. He forgot to go as his father would have done, slowly and carefully; he went chasing down through the bracken and the long grass, forgetting completely that she was with him. But she ran behind him just the same, got to the shore a few steps behind him.

'Out there's an island,' he said, the cold taking his breath away. 'There, over to the right. And there's a place on it called the Christmas House. If we get enough ice we can spend Christmas there, we can stay there.'

He looked at her to see how she'd respond. Her mouth was open, and she was looking, her eyes bright – he didn't need to ask.

'So you'll come, Winifred, if it freezes?'

She looked at him, nodding as though he was stupid.

'And I hate Winifred,' she said. 'Call me Winnie like everyone else.'

•

There was a morning when Lewis drifted in a no-man's land between sleeping and waking. He knew he was not in the boarding house; he knew somewhere deep inside that he was at home. He had worked out the night before that another twelve days of the holiday remained; if he counted the drive back to the station and the train journey too it was twelve and a half. He had gone to sleep with twelve and a half days safe and soft in his head; they rocked him to sleep. And he dreamed that a real winter came, the sort of winter there once had been on earth, when forty or fifty degrees of frost locked everything in a white fist of ice.

He was at Glenellen and the school was caught in a vice-like grip. He walked through corridors rejoicing because there

The Ice and other stories

could be no more classes and everyone had gone. He found himself beside the swimming pool and the water had turned to one piece of solid blue ice. He would never have to learn to swim again. Then, all of a sudden, he turned round and Winnie was there. Her brown eyes held him and she began running. She ran out of the old building and its frozen pool onto the playing fields at the back of Glenellen. She ran into the trees beside the rugby fields and he could see the shape of the Lodge peeping out through the birches. He could see the grey-white shimmer of the lake behind. She had brought him back. . .

He felt someone shaking him and calling his name, but he wanted them to go away, he didn't want to come back from his dream. But they kept pulling at his shoulder, and he opened his eyes to push them away.

'Lewis! Lewis, it's me!' It was his granny, and he knew it was very early in the morning. The room was still half-dark; in the other bed was the unmistakeable hump of Roddy's back. She set a cup of hot orange on his bedside table; he could tell by the scent. That was what she had made for him each morning when his mum was so ill in hospital and he had come back home from school. She had brought him hot orange that stung his lips and tongue, and warmed him all the way to his toes. And she had put her hand through his hair.

He struggled to sit up, his face crumpled with sleep. He could hear her smiling.

'The ice is thick enough. You can go out to the island tonight.'

·

At five o'clock Harry went over the ice. They all went down to
watch, and John Cameron was closest to the shore, the firefly
of his cigarette moving in the blue dark. It was already eight
below. He finished giving instructions about the path that led
to the House, and how to get in, and suddenly there was
silence and Harry set off. His boots thudded on the ice; the
light of his head torch flickered this way and that as his shadow
went out and became part of the night. Lewis thought of the
story of Jesus walking on the water, and at that moment he
realised that what he had dreamed might happen had
happened after all. His father had been wrong; the ice had
come and they were going to the Christmas House, now on
the 23rd of December. Winnie was beside him and he could
catch the scent of her, he was sure of it. He closed his eyes
and felt such a well of happiness deep inside he almost lost
his breath. *This was going to happen*.

'I'm here!' Harry's call reached them; echoed over the
ice and hung there in the utter stillness of the hills. And they
came alive again, the listeners; they shuffled their freezing
feet and murmured things to each other – John Cameron to
his mother with the lantern by the shore, Roddy to Winifred
so she laughed. Harry's head torch flashed in the trees, a single
beam of brightness in the middle of the night. Then, as they
turned to go back to the Lodge, the light was gone too. Lewis
was the last to turn. Harry had found the path.

·

The Ice and other stories

It was Granny Cameron who came down to see them off. Lewis went first because he simply couldn't wait any longer; his bundle of rugs so stacked in his arms he almost couldn't see where he was going, and a kettle clanking from the rucksack on his back. Yet he tried to look all the same; not just ahead to where they were going but all around – up into the hill opposite, silver-plated with moonlight, the pines an eerie white with their jewellery of frost. He caught the wary eyes of four hinds in a clearing low down on the hill; their ears were like bears', little half moons of listening. They watched and then, as if on cue, turned and rustled away into the trees and were gone.

'Don't go so fast! Wait for me!' Winnie protested.

He turned at once, waiting and happy. The Lodge lights cast vague gold trails over the ice. Roddy had barely set out from the shore; he was trying to carry all that was left in one go despite his grandmother's chiding.

'Did you tell your parents?' Lewis suddenly asked her when she'd caught up with him.

'Tell them what?' She kept her eyes on the ice.

'About coming here. That we would come here.'

She shook her head. 'They were busy with everything. I don't remember. Look at Roddy! He can hardly walk!'

Her laughter rang out and echoed, and for just a second Lewis wanted to tell her she was breaking the quiet. She'd turned back a few steps, as though she wanted to share Roddy's burden. Granny Drummond was slowly making her way back up towards the Lodge; she had whispered to him to *remember every second*.

So Lewis and Winnie got to the island first. It was the

little beach he had seen from the top of Croft Hill. He was tempted to drop everything in one great heap and throw himself on top, so aching were his arms, but he bit his tongue and didn't.

They fought their way between branches, trying to follow something that might once have been a path. That was the worst bit. There were things you couldn't see, even in the steel whiteness of the moonlight, and Lewis fought his way forwards, stabbed by sharp bits of branches.

'Thanks, that almost took my eye out!' Winnie told him indignantly as a spray of shadows brushed back against her face. 'Is it much further?'

He didn't answer because suddenly they were there, in a little glade shut in by pine trees and dense undergrowth. They were there and the cabin was right in front of them. A plume of maroon smoke was rising from the little chimney in the middle of the roof; the fire inside popped and whined. Good old Harry.

Getting inside was more difficult. The door had broken and the only thing to do was to crawl in under what was left of it. Lewis looked inside, from the vantage point of his knees. The one long window; the red roar of fire in the grate. They left their burdens outside and crawled in first. Winnie went over to the window and looked out.

'It could be Siberia!' she breathed. 'Look at it, Lewis!'

He stood there with her, his head bent close to hers. It was like a window in an advent calendar, he thought. The moon high in the sky over the trees and the Lodge; then the lake with its silver patternings, a white floor of whorls and paths.

'Can't you imagine wolves?' Winnie said. 'Wolves coming over that, hunting? You feel as if it could be any time, I mean ages ago. Like walking into a story, a story you once read.'

Then Roddy arrived, and for the next forty minutes they were struggling to bring rugs in, to light lamps and make up beds in the little space there was. All their toes would point in to the middle. Roddy built a great stack of wood for the fire, and somehow it smelled like mushrooms. The last thing they did was to barricade the broken door, and then the three of them were lying in the darkness, listening to the roar of the fire in the chimney. Roddy had said he would get up at three to make sure it was still going; he always woke up then anyway, and he would rebuild it so it still had life in the morning.

Lewis didn't want to sleep. He wanted instead to lie in that place between waking and sleeping, the thump and hiss of the fire in his ears. They had got to the island; it had happened.

He fell asleep all the same, though his dreaming felt real enough. He woke and the fire was dead. The Christmas House was filled with silver light; it shone on the face of Winnie who was next to him, and on Roddy who was furthest away. She was facing him, on her side, and she might have been a silver sculpture. He could not even hear the sound of her breathing. He got up and slipped out of the House; he glided across the path of ice towards the Lodge that lay now in darkness, asleep. He went inside and found his fiddle case; he took the violin and went back out into the very middle of the lake and began playing. He stood there playing and all sorts of creatures came alive and gathered at the edge of the frozen lake; the deer came down to listen, and the pine martens with their gorgeous orange tummies, and the long-snouted badgers. And last of all, Winnie came out of the Christmas House, smiling, and he turned towards her, for it had been for her he really wanted to play.

•

The three of them were up at nine. Roddy hadn't woken after all during the night and the fire was a mess of bitter-smelling ash and charred ends of wood. They could see their breath. The cold was sore; it felt as though parts of arms and legs weren't there anymore. Lewis pulled on his clothes, juddering, his fingers like whittled twigs. They didn't speak; even their mouths were locked and sore. Lewis crawled out under the broken door and saw that everything was covered in white as though some giant had breathed on the world in the night. The Lodge was gone; a carpet of mist lay on the lake and hid the mainland from them. He whirled his arms about him and bashed his red hands against his sides. Then he heard Winnie, turned round and saw her standing laughing helplessly at him. He smiled, shy, and the dream came back to him.

It took them thirty-six matches and a great deal of blowing to coax that fire into life. Then, for the next hour, they did little but sit round it in the middle of the room, watching the flames and waiting to thaw.

'What's that box under there?' Winnie asked at last. She'd noticed something under one of the ledges, something they hadn't brought with them over the ice. They looked, reluctant to move. Lewis finally struggled up, his feet still sharp with frost, and slid it out. It was wooden, covered with a layer of dust and ash and fragments of bark. It was like something that had survived a volcano, that belonged to another world entirely. He swept his hand over the top to clear it.

'The Christmas Box,' he read. He brought it over to beside the others, not opening it until he was there. Winnie brought out a velvet bag that rattled; she struggled with the drawstring, then poured into her hand a collection of sheep and shepherds and kings and angels. The three faces peered at them as Winnie spread them between her hands. They were made of white wood and were roughly carved, all about the size of a thumb.

'I bet granddad did those,' Roddy said, leaning over.

'I bet he carved them,' and he glanced at Lewis. 'Gran still has his favourite knife, that one with the mother of pearl handle.'

And Lewis thought of the precious elephant in his pocket, made of the same white wood. He remembered the knife from his gran's bedroom; they had been allowed to pick it up and look at it, but not take it away.

Winnie set the nativity figures on the stonework beside the fire. The light played on the carved figures. There were candles in the box, and one or two very old Christmas cards; half a dozen pinecones that were dry and fragile with age, that weighed as little as air. They brought out everything and found a place for it; they did so in silence and with a kind of puzzled reverence, as the mist swept at last from the lake and the morning turned a fierce white-blue, one single pane of light.

It was Christmas Eve and Granny Cameron brought down a box of skates from the attic. They were her own, and would do for Winnie, and after a lot of rummaging there was a pair for Lewis too. Roddy assured them that he would break a leg and that would mean no cricket for the whole next season; he was still cold and found Tosca and Rascal in the utility room, took them running up Croft Hill.

'Watch that bit at the bottom of the island,' John Cameron called over the ice. 'I'm not sure I'd trust it. Keep to this bit, between the Lodge and the top.'

Lewis heard, but he was calling and whooping. He fell and it hurt but he laughed; he laughed at the blue sky above him and at Winnie's face looking down at his. And Granny Cameron stood at the shore, her arms bound tightly against the frozen light, and she remembered how he had been just two years before – broken and bereft, like a bird that would never fly again. She had not wanted him to go to Glenellen at all; she had fought hard with her son against it. She well knew what was waiting for him there, how ill prepared he was to meet it. But she was never going to have the last word, and she always knew she was set to lose in the end. Yet here he was now, and that was all that mattered.

Later they trailed into the Lodge and drank hot mulled wine from round, green pottery bowls. Roddy came back with Tosca and Rascal and a story of a fox; after that they sat and grazed, as Granny Cameron put it – hot sprouts and ham, hot tea. They sat in front of a fire that would have roasted a musk ox, and outside the light gathered itself to a sheer crystal white,

The Ice and other stories

and Lewis watched it from the window as six woodpigeons ruffled up soundlessly from the trees on the far lake shore and blinked into the whiteness and were gone. His granny was suddenly there beside him.

'May I come over and join you this evening?' she asked. It was his permission she had sought, and he noticed. His face lit up.

'Course you can. If you bring a present.'

She thought for a second. 'Why don't we open all our presents there, all our family ones?'

And so they did. Roddy and Lewis took an arm each because she was frightened of falling; John Cameron came behind with a sledge laden with parcels, and the bottle of his favourite malt which had come from Winnie's parents.

The fire was coaxed into life and the candles lit so a lemony light filled the Christmas House. They blocked the gap in the door as best they could and it felt like being in an igloo. That was what Lewis suddenly thought; it was an igloo.

'We should have had Harry with us,' Granny Cameron said, looking over at her son. 'We could have given him his present here. Still, I expect he's perfectly content to be with his family tonight.'

'And with a large bottle of brandy, if I know Harry Cartwright,' John added. 'What about presents then? If my arms don't have movement soon they're liable to get frostbite. Shall I be Father Christmas?'

Winnie had hers first, since she was the guest. There was a present she knew at once was a book; it was a copy of Swiss Family Robinson, something she had – but this was much nicer-looking, and she didn't let on. The other parcel was soft and small; she squashed it to try to guess.

'They're going to come in pretty handy,' her uncle winked, and that was true. They were sheepskin gloves, and Winnie put them on then and there. They were as good as little ovens.

Roddy got a new satchel for fishing, and examined every pocket and compartment. Granny Cameron had only brought her presents from the boys; Roddy had made her a bird table in woodwork; Lewis a toast rack.

'Your grandfather would be proud of you,' she told them.

'Just don't eat your breakfast from the wrong one,' her son told her, throwing another log onto the fire. 'There's a parcel for you, Lewis, one from me.'

It weighed nothing, was wrapped in grey paper. He opened it carefully, remembering how he used to get a row for tearing the paper.

'For heaven's sake put us out of our misery!' his father said, and Lewis felt his face reddening, thinking of Winnie hearing.

He opened the little box and it was a pair of swimming trunks; blue, with a white stripe down one side.

'For when you can swim! Later this year!'

'You mean next year, dad,' Roddy pointed out.

'All right, whatever, next year.'

Lewis said thank you, but he felt far away, as if someone else was saying the words inside him. He felt like a puppet; he felt as if the real him was getting smaller and smaller inside. The talk around him became one single voice; all the words melted together, became like the sound on a radio when the station isn't clear.

Later that night, when the three island inhabitants had

gone out and said good night to their visitors; after they'd barricaded the door again and built up the fire into a golden dome of flame, he took the swimming trunks and crushed them into the corner of his bag so they were gone, so they weren't there any more.

'Where are you, Lewis?' Winnie asked, tapping his head playfully, as the three of them sipped sweet cocoa in the burning glare of the fire.

'I'm here,' he said, but he knew it wasn't true all the same. He tried with all his might to clamber back into himself and be there, the only place he wanted to be. But he kept falling away; he kept hearing the drip, drip in his head that dragged him back. He kept remembering, and all he wanted to do was forget. His eyes burned when they went to bed at last, and he lay awake hour after hour, long after he yearned to sleep.

•

It was partridge they had that Christmas afternoon, when the Lodge clock had fluttered four times, and they sat round the table at last with its red napkins and white candles. If Lewis were to have craned his neck he'd have been able to see the island there in the bottom left hand corner of the window, but he was much too busy passing roast parsnips and potatoes, and talking to Mrs Jenkins, the widowed piano teacher who lived between the end of the road and the village.

'I've always said that Lewis shouldn't have let his piano lessons go. He was one of the best pupils I had – such promise.'

Granny Cameron looked older. Lewis suddenly realised

that; she was sitting opposite him in her white dress with the topaz brooch that her husband had brought back from Ceylon after his war was over. It glittered like the blue of her eyes, but she was older just the same. He hadn't noticed that before; it was as though it had happened while he was away, and he felt an overwhelming desire to hold her, not to let her go.

'Lewis. Lewis!'

He looked up startled, met his father's gaze.

'Mrs Jenkins was asking what stage you've reached with the violin! Are you still with us?'

Roddy and Winnie and he drank cider. It gave him an orange taste in his mouth, mingled with the partridge and flowed into his head. He watched Winnie as she sat talking to his father; he was leaning close to her and she was nodding, her brown eyes bright. He knew he should look away but he couldn't, and then she seemed to know and she glanced at him and their eyes met. Just a flash and he looked away, shy, and she and his father were laughing. He wanted there to be time; to go up into the wood on the other side of the lake to look for red squirrels, to take her up Croft Hill and let her find the deer with the monocular. If there was enough moonlight they could go sledging away up behind the Lodge. . . Suddenly he realised he didn't want Roddy to be there and he felt bad. He only wanted this to last for ever, to go back and back over the ice to the Christmas House and the fire and the night.

The pudding was borne in by Roddy, its blue ghosts of flames blown out as he set it down in the middle of the applause.

'Should you be having brandy butter?' his father teased

Winnie, jogging her elbow. 'All this alcohol, you're going to go home swaying to Manchester!'

'And you're going to go swaying out to your pheasant pens next Monday morning!' his mother retorted, her whole face crinkling. 'I think you've very few stones to throw!'

'Guilty as charged!' He raised his hands in mock surrender, and Mrs Jenkins told them of an occasion when an elderly minister had arrived at the house for a piano lesson, rather the worse for wear.

'Poor man, it was Christmas. I think he'd had mulled wine from every guild and choir in the parish!'

Later they went through to the sitting room that flowed with Beethoven. Mrs Jenkins' fingers rippled along the sleeve of her other hand as she listened, marvelling at the waterfalling notes. Lewis sat, leaning in to the fire in the cold silk of his shirt and tie. Roddy sat cross-legged between the couch and his grandmother, biting his nails. Lewis knew he was restless; he'd want to be off out with Tosca and Rascal, but he knew what his father would say.

'Gran, can I get something from the island?'

Lewis had suddenly remembered the Christmas box that Winnie had found; he wanted to show her the figures his grandfather had carved. She might never have seen them before. . .

'Of course, on you go. Mrs Jenkins has to get home soon, though, so come straight back and I'll make tea. No, please do stay, Joan!'

He went down to the lake running, his feet hissing through the white bracken. He ran straight out onto the ice and he saw how the sky ahead was a mingling of white and blue and yellow. Suddenly he wished he could paint, he wished he could have captured that light. He stopped, there in the middle of that pathway of ice, gulping the air into his chest. He wanted to walk into that light, to walk into it and never stop.

He brought back everything in the end; somehow he wanted it to be exactly as when Winnie had found it and opened it. He wanted his grandmother to see just what it had been like. But when he came out of the Christmas House on his hands and knees, the box held awkwardly in front of him, the air was dark blue and the light had gone. He had only been a minute or two and yet it had gone.

The box was heavier than he had thought it would be. It banged sore against his thighs as he carried it back and he had to walk slowly; he felt every step as he trudged up the hillside to the Lodge.

'Lewis?'

He hadn't seen his father in the shadows; he jumped with fright, didn't reply. His father had come out for a smoke.

'I want you to come back to the house tonight. It's going to be milder by the morning. After Mrs Jenkins has gone you can go over and bring all your stuff back.'

The words echoed inside him. He felt his face burn with anguish and frustration and anger. He didn't hear his own words as he railed at the back of his father retreating to the Lodge. It wasn't fair, it was wrong, he couldn't. His words melted into crying, into a tangle of angry sobs and words that no longer made any sense. He chucked the box on the ground and crouched down, folded into himself, weeping as he'd done when he was four. He couldn't take this away; it wasn't

The Ice and other stories

his and he didn't have the right. He didn't care. He hugged his arms about his chest and blinked down, searching, to the lake. But the island was gone, swallowed by dark.

•

Now the Lodge was quiet; all the lights were out. Roddy's soft snore was like a whine; along the corridor their father had gone to bed at last. Lewis had heard Winnie closing her door and he had not been able to put her out of his mind. He remembered her scent and sat there on the floor in the darkness, thinking. Then he thought of the Christmas House and he glanced away, wanting to escape the prison of his own thoughts. He would drive himself mad. He had left last; by then Roddy had been out onto the ice with his heap of rugs and boxes, calling back impatiently for him to hurry. He hadn't had time to say goodbye. . .

And there on the floor beside him were the swimming trunks. Their white stripe showed in the darkness of the room. He felt himself back at Glenellen on a morning in mid-October. He could hear Macgregor. . .

'All right, there's room for an awful lot of improvement; I'm pretty disappointed with most of you. Now, I have to be at a meeting in exactly eight and a half minutes, so out in two and shower. Ditchfield, you are my eyes and ears. One scrap of trouble and I want to know. Understood?'

'Yes, sir.'

The plimsolls squeaked along the changing room corridor as Macgregor disappeared. Again there was the sound of the ticking drip of water. Then the outer door banged and the place hurt with the echoes of shrieking and laughter, the sound of water being cuffed and bodies dive-bombing the deep end. Ditchfield was shouting something at George Fife; shouting was the only way of making yourself heard. If only he'd come back, Lewis thought. If only he could hear.

But he didn't. In a couple of minutes they began dragging themselves from the water, knowing the period bell was looming. As Lewis was clambering out at the shallow end, he felt hands at his shoulders pulling him backwards. For a confused second he saw a sea of faces above him as he was dunked in the water; their piercing shrieks hurt his ears as he went under and struggled up, fighting his way through them and gasping for breath.

'Cameron, where d'you get your trunks? Your mother?'

The showers were already on when he got out of the pool. He could hear someone singing, then the sound of someone else farting. That started the rest of them on underarms farts, the loudest and the best. He went back to his cubicle as slowly as he could, dragged down his sodden black trunks and picked up his towel. He could hear his heart in his chest. He walked back into the sweat and the steam.

'Here he comes, lads! Make way for the great athlete! Oh, I think you've dropped a muscle, Cameron. Aren't you going to pick it up?'

He saw Ditchfield ahead of him, a whole head taller than himself. He was looking at him with nothing less than hatred. His eyes were black.

'What's that between your legs, Cameron? Is it real or is it just stuck on? Here, shall we find out, lads?'

Ditchfield had whipped down his towel from a hook at

the side of the showers. Some of the jackals started clapping, cheering and clapping. On the other side and out of the corner of his eye, Lewis saw another towel whipped down. He glanced at the clock, willing the minute hand to move. There was still another four and a half minutes to the bell. They'd trapped him. He couldn't get back to his own towel.

Ditchfield dipped the end of his in the water and twisted it round, taking all the time he wanted. He practised a flick, letting the towel crack in the air in front of him. The slow clapping increased; the murmur of expectation and delight. Ditchfield moved closer.

A towel came at Lewis from another corner and he reached out pathetically with his right hand. He felt the cold gust of air. A loud echo of mirth went up at his attempt to save himself. He glanced at Ditchfield, his eyes pleading now. He felt his own back against a cold shower top. He couldn't go any further.

Ditchfield took aim at his groin and Lewis clutched at himself. The wet tongue of towel stung against his hands and was gone. How many seconds were there to the bell? How many seconds were there to go? The other towel came to distract him again and he swung round, enraged and humiliated. At the same time, Ditchfield took aim. The lightning fork flickered in the air and there was an audible crack as it hit. Lewis screamed and crumpled forward onto the tiles. A cheer rang out and echoed through the whole building.

Ditchfield turned to get dressed, waving his towel in victory. And as they melted away, the bell rang at last.

He held the trunks in his hands. If he reckoned there were thirty weeks of term each year, and he had two periods of swimming a week, that meant three hundred before he left Glenellen. There was no way out.

He heard something, a muffled sound from Winnie's room, and he held his breath. It was ten past twelve; Christmas Day was gone. He listened and realised that Winnie was crying. It was like a soft, slow wave; it was like the way he had cried when his mother had died and he simply lay on his gran's couch hour after hour. He had thought then of a story, the story of a child whose mother dies and who goes down to the underworld to ask if ever she might be restored. Oh yes, was the answer, if you weep a whole river of tears, and that river flows down here into the darkness, she will be restored. So he went back and wept until the river was sufficient. But it wasn't true.

Lewis got up, the swimming trunks still in his hand. He held the door handle, turned it degree by degree so it wouldn't break the hum of the house's quiet. He knew how to do it right; the door sighed open and he went out into the corridor on soft feet. He listened for only a second outside Winnie's door, seeing there was no edge of light showing from inside. He didn't knock, just turned the handle and slid the door open.

She sat up in bed, trying to smudge away her tears.

'I heard you crying,' he breathed, and sat down at the very bottom of the bed. He began to see her face; she grew out of the dark.

'I'm sorry,' she whispered, but he shook his head. That wasn't what he had meant, that wasn't why he had come.

She looked down for a second, into the net of her hands. Then she met his eyes again.

'I was crying because of my mum and dad. I don't want to go home because I know what's there. This was like a dream, and now it's over. They're getting a divorce, and I have to go and live with my mother in America. She's going back there.'

Lewis nodded and felt something break inside him. There was something he had dared hope, or dared begin to hope – like a bridge, or like ice even. He had dared believe he could walk over, that it would hold, and now too that was breaking. He was sinking and he could not even cry out.

'When I go home, I have to begin packing. I have to get ready for a whole new world.'

Suddenly he thought of something, one small thing. He searched in his pocket and brought out the little elephant his grandfather had carved. He held it in his fingers, then stretched over, dropped it into her empty hands.

'That's for you,' he said. 'For whenever you're really low, can't go on. Hold it and believe. Never forget.'

He half stood and then he bent forwards through the soft dark of the room and laid his cheek against hers, just and no more. He caught her scent and closed his eyes.

'Goodbye,' he whispered.

'Goodbye,' she breathed, not understanding, her word more like a question. And then he had gone; before she could speak the words in her heart he had turned away. It was as though he swam through the room's shadow, and flowed out of her world into somewhere else, and she had to touch her cheek to believe he had been there at all.

He went downstairs, his hand a hiss on the wood of the banister. In the porch he found his shoes and slipped them on. It was raining; a fine rain as thin as soft hair, covering the woods and the Hallion hills. He turned and went round the side of the track, started down the slope towards the lake through the frost-sculpted grass and bracken. They jagged his ankles like tiny swords. Just once he looked back, up at Granny Cameron's window, but it was dark and empty, like a blind eye.

He didn't stop; he went on down to the bottom and out over the ice, the way Harry had taken that first day. He looked for the Christmas House but it was lost in the dark and the rain, as if it had never been. He went on, his feet making not a sound, until he'd reached the rocks at the end of the island. The ice creaked. He smiled and stopped, began taking off his clothes until he stood sculpted white and pure in the moonlight. Then he put on the new trunks.

# Conquering

**1962. It was the autumn Mrs Giggs broke my mother's** favourite vase. It was the autumn Charlie Rutherford ran away with the woman who owned the Tower Hotel. And it was the autumn my parents sat glued to the television because of some international row over pigs. I couldn't understand why everyone was getting so worked up about the Russians and some pigs. One evening my mother was even dabbing her eyes as she came out of the living room, and when my father finally switched off the little black and white box, and come out and shut the door soundlessly behind him, it was as though he had closed the door on a funeral.

I wasn't the least bit interested. I was eight years old and the only thing that worried me about pigs was that Craig and I might not get our bacon rolls on Friday evening when he came round to play Scrabble. We always had bacon rolls and piping hot tea at eight o'clock when he arrived, and if my mother were to go back on that, there would be *repercussions*. I had no idea what repercussions were, but everyone who spoke about this business of the Russians and these pigs said there were going to be serious repercussions. I had the word in my head the whole time and I enjoyed rolling it round my mouth like a bit of toffee. There were going to be serious repercussions if my mother stopped making those bacon rolls on a Friday evening.

The only thing that put all thought of bacon and Russians and everything else out of my head was Mrs Murray. She arrived on a Thursday at ten past four for my piano lesson and reversed the Gulf Stream when she came down the front hall. With one look that woman could put icicles on the inside of an oven.

'Now, Michael, I hope you've been practising your chromatic scale and haven't been distracted by world events.' She was on about pigs, too! I hadn't been the least bit distracted but that didn't mean I'd been practising as much as she thought. She put that horrible metronome above the piano and it began tutting away like some disapproving Victorian grandfather. Mrs Murray sat there, her lips pursed and her eyes furious, looking like a kettle that was about to boil over. It was scales and rapped knuckles and tutting for an hour and fifteen minutes. Well, for an hour. That last Thursday of the month I could only *half* listen to Mrs Murray for the last quarter of an hour because I was listening to something else. The wind was scurrying round the house, wild and rising.

•

At school Miss Aston said there were just two things that distracted young children – the wind and the moon. She said that a full moon was the worse of the two; it wasn't just children that were affected, it was prisoners, too. When there was a full moon they would get angry and riot and even break out, and we sat in our rows in class and saw prisoners with red eyes and bunching muscles, full of the moon.

The wind was the second thing and that was worse with children. David Scott put up his hand and said his father suffered with the wind but Miss Aston shook her head and said that this wind got into *children* and made them like kites. They flew all over the place and it was especially bad in the autumn. She said they might as well close all primary schools in the autumn because everything went in one ear and was blown out the other. And we sat with our arms folded watching Miss Aston, believing that if she said it the words must be true. Because it didn't matter whether Miss Aston told us about trees in winter or people in the Stone Age; if Miss Aston said it then it must be true.

And that Thursday I heard the wind growing and rising about the house and I thought of what she'd said. And Mrs Murray's words faded like a radio that's been turned down. In my mind's eye I saw Russians with red eyes, full of the wind and angry. There were repercussions and they went round and round my head, echoing and thudding, and I wondered if there would be a seriously big storm, one that cut the electricity and meant we had to use the real fire and candles. The metronome went and Mrs Murray went, and the ice in the front porch melted.

'That woman really does chill the blood,' my father

murmured to me sympathetically, out of earshot of my mother, and clapped my shoulder. Then he disappeared back into the living room, to the television and the six o'clock news.

That night I dreamed of Miss Aston. She was talking about a great storm that was coming, telling us we had to be ready for the great storm. She showed us a map of Britain and said the storm would sweep across the whole country, and across America and Russia, too. We had to be ready for the storm.

I woke up with a start and remembered the chestnuts. The wind was rolling about the house in long waves and I got up and went to the window. There in the night blue sky was a full moon, and I thought that the prisons would be empty that night, for those were the two worst things there could be, a full moon and a high wind. But at that moment the only thing that mattered was the chestnuts. I thought of the big tree at the top of the hill and my heart thudded in my chest like a metronome. It was four in the morning and I was wide awake; there was no point trying to go back to sleep now.

I pulled on my clothes and opened the door. The wind and the moon were everywhere; light shone into the spare room, a blue milk light flickered over the floor. The wind was a vandal, a madly exuberant child rushing around corners and chasing down streets. I knew then that Miss Aston was right; I could *feel* she was right. I had to run myself, right that moment. I had to run all the way to that tree.

I was blown up the hill. It's the only time I've felt it, the wind behind me almost lifting me off my feet. It was as though a wild horse galloped at my back, then slipped underneath me and lifted me into the saddle. I galloped with the wind; I felt I was part of the wind myself. Everything was chasing and dancing. It was neither night nor day; the world was made of blue milk, but I could have run for miles and never needed a light. I could see the clouds scudding overhead; I could see the trees on the far hill, tossing their heads in a wild, mad sea. I wanted to be up among them; I wanted to climb the highest of them and feel the wind rippling and roaring in the branches. I wanted to be tossed from side to side and to look out from the very top, to see the whole of the storm. This was the biggest thing I had ever known.

The wind horse set me down at the top of the hill. There was a lull. There wasn't a breath of wind where I was. But I heard other great and terrible booms from other hills, and I realised for the first time that the wind wasn't just one thing, it was many. And it gave me a thrill and I thought how I'd tell Miss Aston. I'd tell her there wasn't just one wind but there were many and she'd be pleased and smile at me and believe me. I listened to the many winds in the woods and I felt the thrill of each one of them. My heart sang and the wind came back into my wood and I closed my eyes and smiled.

Then I went over the field to the chestnut tree. And for the first time in my life I felt big; I felt as though the wind had made me strong. I wasn't afraid of anything and I decided I was going to go home that day and, whatever else I did, I was going to tell my mother I wasn't going to play the piano any more. Mrs Murray and her metronome would never come back to the house and my life would be utterly happy, for it was the only thing that really got under my skin – Thursday afternoons and piano. But that one thing cast a very long shadow; by Tuesday morning I was dreading the next lesson. I could feel the days of the week by where I was with that piano practice. And now I was going to be brave enough to say I wouldn't play any more, and at that moment I really believed they'd listen, that I'd win. And I ran across the field and the tree with its great ancient branches got bigger and bigger, that dark green canopy of five-fingered leaves filling and heaving with the might of the wind.

•

I got there and I was the first there. They were falling all around me, lacquered things – they made heavy thuds in the wet ground and I darted from one to the next, filling my pockets until they bulged. But high up was one massive conker at the end of a branch, and that was the one I wanted. All the others were also-rans; they didn't count compared with that single conker. I wanted it so badly it hurt and my hands itched. Nothing else mattered except that.

I flung up sticks and they tickled the leaves and fluttered back down to the ground. I even threw stones up, something we had been told never to do after Terry McBride got his own stone back on his forehead and a face shining with blood. But even the rocks I flung rolled down and were lost in the bushes. And my heart hammered as I watched that one chestnut rising and falling in the wind. I would have to climb the tree. And I, who was afraid of heights, who had never climbed a wall let alone a tree, went up into the branches that crazy morning before dawn. I was full of the wind, I was part of the wind; there was nothing I couldn't do. I was going to go home and tell them I'd never play the piano again, that Mrs Murray and the metronome were over. I'd tell them that Thursdays were my own.

And I climbed into the tree and could feel it lifting and breathing with wind. It was as though I was in the rigging of a great ship and I held on till my hands were raw. I fought my way upwards until I held the branch with the conker, and I shook it and rattled it until at last it broke off and I heard it bang down onto the ground. There it lay in front of me, a whole green helmet, and my hands trembled as I lifted it. One edge was open; I could see the polished leather of the conker inside. The shell was as big as my hand.

I opened it and a conker huge as the Kohinoor rolled over my palm. I was too tired to run now; I walked all the way home. But as I walked it was as though the wind blew out of me. The storm was passing and I felt small again; I remembered I was only eight years old. I felt strange and small, and by the time I came to the front door I was not brave any longer. And I thought of Columbus and how it must have been to come back home after finding America.

But when Craig came that evening my mother brought us bacon rolls. She said that things were better in the world again and I took it that meant the trouble with pigs was over. She said too that Mrs Murray had called and was ill and was going to have to cancel my lessons for the time being, and that meant a thousand times more. I held the conker in my hand and felt happy beyond words. I heard the last of the wind round the house and knew that somehow I had won after all.

# Teddy Fry

**Mrs Able gave him blackcurrant and apple sweets. Miss Ruby**
Allan (she stressed the *Miss* like an adder enraged in heather)
had so many ailments but had to count her blessings because
of her nephew Toby, and Matthew Macdonald did not eat pork.
Everyone who ever visited Adler House knew that.

Danny Kilbride realised after only a week of working there
that he liked Teddy Fry best. He sat in his wheelchair beside
the windows at the far end of the west wing of Adler House.
He wore a suit that was soft black and shining as if made of
moles, and every day a fresh cravat adorned his neck, blue
and gold like the colour of a dragonfly's wings, or red as a
kestrel's back. He had his paper folded on his knees when
Danny came in but he never seemed to be reading. He held
his round tortoiseshell glasses in the thin stem of his right
hand and the blue veins bulged.

*Good morning*. His voice was nothing more than a whisper, but his head inclined, his eyes lit and shone like suns. Danny's heart thudded in his chest when he cleaned Teddy Fry's room. He spent five whole minutes polishing the sink and made sure every layer of the bed was folded down smoothly and equally. Once he was so absorbed in cleaning the spots from the mirror that Mrs MacEchnie told him to *move his arse* to Ruby's room. He looked involuntarily at Teddy Fry when she said that, the duster clenched in his hands, his face growing hot and pink. But Teddy Fry was looking out into the sunlight of the spring morning, smiling, as a robin and two chaffinches fought over crumbs on the patio stones. He was smiling as if he was far away and the sun played on the black sheen of his suit and on his cravat and over the long white bone of his face.

Ruby wasn't well at all; she breathed as if she was trying to climb something and kept falling back. Danny had known she was going to get worse; he had known it when he bought the *Daily Record* last Saturday afternoon at the newsagents on the corner of Portland Street when the fifty pence of his change flashed in the light.

It was always in the nape of his neck, that feeling. It had been the same when his mother's friend, Mrs Copeland, told them she had lung cancer and when his brother's oldest pal, Mitchell, broke his neck diving during the long copper heat of 1976. It was always in the nape of his neck, a feeling like a hand lifting the thin gold hair there backwards, on end. Because he had known it already. . .

'Bloody well die then, can you no'?' Irene Scott moaned and squelched the mop into her bucket that morning, as the clouds blackened like brambles and the rain sang in choirs on the old tin roofs in the gardens.

'Ah'm dyin' for a fag,' Maggie Stuart hissed and she shifted the position of her feet yet again as she leaned across the nurses' table, watching Ruby Allan's room for some sign that it was all over at last. Danny's heart was going like a smith's hammer; he wanted to shout but he couldn't. The words shrivelled in his mouth always, just before he had the courage to utter them, like dark green ivy leaves. They lay dried and sour in his stomach when at last Ruby was wheeled away for ever and they went in with their mops and polishers to take away the smell of death, to make the lies white and shining and lovely once again.

It was the following Saturday when he found Teddy Fry's diary. He was on his own that day; Mrs MacEchnie had bronchitis and Nancy (who was always asking if he didn't go to the cinema) was cleaning the rooms over in the east wing. Danny had reached up to dust a shelf Mrs MacEchnie had expressly told him he didn't need to bother with; he brushed against the heavy book and it thudded onto the wooden floor. He glanced at Teddy Fry; the old man was asleep in his wheelchair, the polished white of his head bent forwards into the early March light as if in prayer. His paper had fallen softly as a sigh from his knees.

The diary had opened as it fell. There was nothing on the cover but the faded gold of the date – 1934. Danny reached for it with trembling reverence, crouched as he lifted it and turned it over. He did not mean to read it, he would never. . . It was the *writing* he marvelled at first; the sheer grace of the inked letters as they flowed like swans across their lines. They were unnecessary curves, superfluous to requirement, wasteful even. He thought for a second of Mrs MacEchnie's notes, and of the scribbled anger of his mother's sticky labels left on fridges and above the dog's slobberings at the back door.

This writing gave him a feeling inside that he could only think afterwards was like autumn; it reminded him of looking into a deep September wood from far away and seeing just a swathe of it lit with beams of liquid lemon and red. It made you want to reach it before that light faded, for you could not be sure it would ever be quite the same again. But to get closer he had to read the words. . .

I am so glad for Johannes'company. We drove up
from Oxford yesterday and the whole way he was
telling me about his thesis on Thomas Mann and
his symbolism, and it chimes in perfectly with all
I've been writing on Ibsen! The light, the light's
just the same. I simply can't believe I've found him.
We arrived at Garth just after four and simply never
wanted to stop talking. Even Emma noticed – my
own little sister watching me like a hawk – I'll have
to be careful. And yet I don't care, I only want this
to last. All my life I've been running to get somewhere, and suddenly I know it's here, it's this. . .
It was exactly as I hoped it would be when he came
here. I feel as if somehow I'd put all of it together
myself. The sun just perfect; at that angle behind
the trees so everything's spangled like in an
Impressionist painting. Yes, even Johannes said it

The Ice and other stories

reminded him of something of Monet's. The pool
had leaves on it but we swam anyway; it was warm
until late, just that wonderful gold in the skies
lingering and lingering. Behind the gates there
were apples; they must have blown in during the
gales last autumn. They were light as feathers but
they'd kept their colour, as if by magic.
The Ashwells must have been having a dance at the
house. I kept on praying Johannes wouldn't ask if
we could go – the music seemed to fill the lawns in
blue shadows and we could hear laughter like soft
glass in the trees. But he just smiled and kept
there, half under the water – he was gold, like a
god. I told him I wanted to come to Germany, that I
wanted him to take me to Lake Constance, to
Bavaria. He said he would take me flying in his
father's plane, that we could go down to
Kandinsky's country and the Austrian Alps.
I felt almost that we were in our own golden bell of
light, that all we struggle for in this damned world
of ours, all we fight against and rage at, broke for
one moment to let us through. Our own Eden. For
as long as I breathe on this earth I swear I will not
forget that light. . .

Danny put the book back as soft as a whisper. But all that
day its pictures waltzed with him, they flurried like wild-blown
leaves through his head till he was giddy, till his heart
hammered. He ran all the way home through the grey chatter
of the rain, but not only because he had no coat. His father

was watching wrestling in the living room and the moment he saw his mother he knew they had been rowing. He heard it in her footsteps, saw it in her forehead. . .

His hands were trembling to find the map, the one his grandfather had given him. He ploughed through comics and cigarette cards and action men in the attic until he had it. One of those maps made of cloth, that fell open like moths' wings. His eyes took it in greedily, could not focus on one place, but went chasing over the sites of wells and chapels and stone circles and Roman roads. But all that day only one word had whispered through his blood and he hungered after it, his eyes begged to find it. He knew he had heard it somewhere before and yet he could not remember where or when; it was locked in the secret box of his memory and the key to it was rusty and useless. *Garth*. There; he fell on the Gothic letters and a warm sea of gladness flooded his chest.

He went the following morning. The skies had torn after the rain, they were filled with blue lace. The roads were scoured and shining; the wheels of his bicycle hissed as they spun. It took him a lot longer than he imagined; he went wrong twice and had to ask at a farm where two little girls like ducklings wandered about barefoot in shallow puddles and insisted on giving him pinecones.

But he got there. He walked the last of the way uphill, listening to the bicycle's tick as he recovered his breath and watched a rainbow melt over the valley. Three woodpigeons rattled away from the beech trees beside him as he stopped and saw the avenue that led straight to the brow of the hill.

*Garth*. The sign was muffled like a green man's face in a bank of moss and fronds, and underneath, the letters that told it was a private road had half fallen away. He walked on, still slower, listening and letting his eyes circle the trees – breathing, thinking, wondering.

The glass of the windows was broken. It was almost as though the house's eyes had been put out. Danny let his bicycle splay down in the long grass, the wheels whirring. A sundial the colour of pantiles had toppled into the middle of the lawn, yet the rockeries remained all but intact, only overgrown with wild green and brown beards. The boy walked softly, so softly, just as he walked over the floor in Teddy Fry's room.

On the other side of the house he stopped. There had been gates there, made of wood, but they had been broken and rotten for long enough from the look of them. Behind was a pool surrounded by tiles, and up above there must at one time have been a dome with glass to let through the sun. Danny looked at it for a long time and then he turned to the gates. Under them and around them were deep piles of leaves, not only last year's but autumn upon autumn of leaves, and in among them apples. The dried ghosts of apples.

He looked up, suddenly, as if he had sensed something. He saw it at once, standing on the edge of a small ridge to the east of the house, an upright ledge of stone. He wandered out from the wreckage of the tiles and went towards it, his feet leaving a silver trail through the grass.

JOHANNES VON ELMAU
who died somewhere in the skies
above Germany, 1944.
May the angels have caught him
before he fell.

There was a picture engraved above the inscription, of two boys leaping, throwing a ball between them. Danny bent as close as he could, leaning his hand on the top of the stone, and he thought that the ball was the sun.

It was at that moment he was sure he felt it, the dark touch at the nape of his neck. He stood tall as if jolted upright. He turned round to gaze at the old ruin of Garth, but it did not come from there, he was sure. Then he knew, he knew without a shadow of a doubt.

He clattered onto the bicycle, spun down the track with his legs flailing. At Rumbling Bridge he all but skidded into an oncoming Land Rover, but he mounted once more and pedalled on, hearing the huge grapes of rain falling around him from the overhanging branches of the oaks. He cycled as fast as he could and yet he was not sure it would be enough; he prayed to the God he no longer believed in that he would not be too late, that time still remained.

He cycled over the deep gravel of the driveway to Adler House and was shouting already, though he did not rightly know the words that babbled from his mouth. He burst through the double doors and ran through the corridor, a whiff of Mrs Able's sweets ripe in his nostrils. He could already see Maggie Stuart now leaning impatient over her bucket in the corridor; he could hear Mrs MacEchnie telling them what had to be cleaned and in what order. He banged against Irene Scott and fell over. They shouted at him but they were underwater, all of them, and they swam at him without touching him. The nurses were in the room, three of them bending over the man in his wheelchair. Danny saw the white ovals of their faces for a split second as they stood back, and he ran at them, his mouth still open with accusations and crying.

He grasped the handles of the wheelchair. He drove it forward into the single pane of the window and out onto the patio. The air was filled with splinters of diamonds; they covered Teddy Fry's hair and his hair, they filled their hands and clothes like priceless confetti. And the low sun broke through the clouds, the light shone like a golden bell, came to bless the face of Teddy Fry.

The Ice and other stories

# Lemon Ice Cream

**If I close my eyes now, very tightly, I can smell everything.**
The ice cream that my father is scooping into bowls in green-
white curves, the little kitchen with its open dishes of herbs
and its baskets of vegetables. The windows are open and all
of us – my mother, my brother, my father and me – we are all
looking out onto the umber sea of the fields, and the scent
that is coming in is from the lemon grove.

I used to get up early in the summer to walk there, just to
be there. To lie on my back and listen to the shingling of the
leaves and let that scent, the scent of the lemons, fill me
completely. And at night when I couldn't sleep in my tiny
room under the attic, I would open the latch of the windows
and let in the lemon breath of the dark.

I was four years old. Born in Sicily under the shadows of
the mountains. My father called Mount Etna *the blue ghost*.
And when I was five we left, all of it was taken away as suddenly

and completely as a teacher wiping a blackboard. There were little finches my father fed; they came to one of the windows at the very top of the farmhouse and he fed them. Most of the other boys had grown to love hunting such birds; netting them and caging them. But my father had a soft heart; he could not bear to see such beautiful things hurt, and he fed the finches. It was the last thing we did before we left, him and me; we stood there with our palmfuls of seeds, me stretching on tiptoe, the tears on my face. His voice was so soft; those words of kindness he whispered both to the finches and to me. They were for both the finches and me.

We were leaving for America, for New York. It was a time of new hope, new dreams, and no dreams came bigger than America. And the last thing my father took from that farmhouse, that place that had been home to six generations of our family, was the recipe for lemon ice cream. I don't know where it had been hidden all that time; it was as though like a magician he snapped his fingers and brought it out from behind his ear. But there it was, in an old square envelope, with flowing writing on the front. And his dark brown eyes shone as he showed me.

We sailed to America. Everything we could carry was stowed beneath us in this great ship ploughing towards the New World. Marco and I ran everywhere – he was nine and I was five. This was our Ark; we had set out across the sea for a new world and everything we needed was onboard. We went down as deep into the ship as we could, to beside the great engines that roared and shook like angry dinosaurs. We went up to the highest deck and watched the grey swaying of the sea, and the brown smoke fluttering from the funnel.

•

And we smelled New York before we saw it. We smelled it and we heard it, Marco and I. Very early one morning when the sea had become a pale piece of glass, we scurried up from our cabin, went on deck and leaned out, and we smelled and we heard New York. It was such a mixture of scents, such a tumbling of things, as though an old bin full of rubbish had rolled down the side of a hill. You tried to catch things at random and always it went on rolling. The bin never stopped tumbling out of control, for ever. Hot smells and sour smells and burnt smells and fresh smells and dead smells and new smells. They made us excited, they set us on fire, but my father hushed us as he leaned out too, for he was listening to New York – he was hearing the city.

'Those are the biggest sounds in the world,' he whispered to us, and somehow we believed him that they must be, that they were. He quietened us with those words, he made us listen, and the smells and the sounds gave us pictures in our heads – pictures in ochre and bright green and orange. But when we came to New York a fine rain was falling, a mist like a mesh of flies that seemed to dampen the scents and the sounds and leave only the great looming greyness of the skyscrapers.

We came to our new home, four flights above the street. On the other side of the hall were the Pedinskis, and above us there was nothing but the roof space and the sky. The only place we had to play was the stairs, and we made it our train station, the launch-pad for our rockets, our cave system, our battlefield. On four flights of stairs were Jewish children, Polish children, Italian children and German children. We had nothing but our imaginations and the days were not long enough. We ate each other's food and we never went hungry.

One Saturday in the hot summer we had been outside, all of us children. We came back panting, full of stories, and sat on different stairs, leaning against the wall. My father came out with bowls of lemon ice cream, his ice cream, and as soon as I bent my head to that bowl I smelled home. I was back in the kitchen, I was up feeding the finches, and I was down in the lemon grove. The tears flowed from my eyes and he comforted me. He rocked me in his arms that evening until I fell asleep.

He kept the recipe behind the old carriage clock in the living room. That brown, crinkled envelope. Sometimes if there was a high wind in the autumn, the fall, and the draught crept under the front door and through the top of the high windows, I would hear it rattling behind the clock, dry like an ancient seed pod. It was there behind the clock, the clock that never lost a second's time, that flickered its passing segments of time like hurrying feet. The clock and the paper.

•

Then, one spring, my mother fell ill. Everything was beginning again, coming alive, after the long winter, and it was as though she went the wrong way and couldn't come back. It was as if we kept moving and had to watch her getting further and further away, disappearing into the snow. I remember her waving to me as I set off for school in the morning. The pale oval of her face behind the glass, trying so hard to smile. That is how I saw her, that was the last memory of her every day, that painting of the pain of her smile. I remember going with Marco and my father to pray for her in a little chapel at the heart of the city. I tried so hard to pray but my head was full of the evening traffic, the shouting and laughter outside. I wanted so desperately to guard her and keep her safe from harm in that place, but not even there was there sanctuary.

My father seemed to grow old in front of us after she died. I remember thinking that one night when we sat together in the living room: *the clock and my father were set at different speeds*. One night I had a dream, a particularly vivid dream. It was of a field, a great wide field. I could see nothing beyond it, it was the only thing there was.

And I came on my father in that field and he was planted in the ground. Mad as that sounds now, he was planted in the ground. And I began digging out his hands and feet, his wrinkled fingers and toes, and all the time I was thinking to myself – *this soil is wrong*.

I was twelve years old. Marco had left school and couldn't find a job. My father, who had worked on scaffolding high above the city, who had sat and laughed with friends on beams the width of a leg half a mile over the streets, he had grown afraid. He had lost the courage to put one foot in front of the other.

That winter the snow fell and fell and fell. The skies were quieter than silence itself and the flakes spun like ballerinas from the sky and buried the world in white. The noise of the city diminished bit by bit; like a great, old animal New York lurched into its own cave and went to sleep.

The wind fluttered the curtains in the living room. It was

six o'clock in the morning and I stood there alone, twelve years old and hungry. My father and Marco were asleep. There was nothing left in the house to eat. The wind came again and I shivered; there was a rattling and it was the old envelope behind the clock, the recipe for lemon ice cream. I felt sadder than ever before in my whole life; it was as though there was only one colour in the world now, the colour grey. And I made up my mind. I felt behind the clock and I found the piece of paper. I put on my shoes and I went out into the grey, sleeping morning with that crumpled paper held tight in my left hand.

·

And I sold it, I say no more than that I sold it. I do not even want to think of the people to whom I went, nor the place where that was. All of it still hurts too much; it is like some red sore where new skin will never grow again. It is enough to say that I was paid a bundle of dirty notes. I caught the smell of them as I took them and I felt sick. It was the smell of the subway, the smell of the basement where no light ever reached. All the way home my hands smelled of it too, and I wanted to wash them clean, I wanted to scour them until it was no more.

Even as I came inside I felt sick, but not only with that terrible smell. I felt sick with something else and I sat by the window; I hunched there and cried and cried and cried.

Outside, the new day was just beginning, there were voices and sounds and scents. The first light came red and beautiful through the streets; beams that crept and changed all the time.

The Ice and other stories

And when I stopped crying at last I looked down on all of this and I thought: *the snow and the light are bigger, they are bigger than all of us together*. For there were men toiling in the snow, digging out cars and pushing them and swearing at one another and at their wives. Taxi drivers in their yellow cabs were shaking their fists and yelling. They were blinded by the red light that came low through the city; they tried to shield their eyes and they had to stop. All they could do was shout and swear, and I looked down on them from where I was four flights above, and they seemed so small and what they struggled against so huge.

I looked up and listened; I listened to the one room and I listened to myself. I felt utterly empty. I had cried myself dry; my eyes were empty caves. The dirty banknotes lay strewn over my lap and some were scattered over the floor at my feet. They were like leaves that had blown in the window – old, dead leaves.

My father and brother would be up soon, my father to sit there in the living room and look at pictures and wait, just wait; and my brother to drag on his coat and go out into a city that did not want him.

Except that everything had changed now. I looked up and I listened and I realised I could hear nothing at all. The clock had stopped ticking.

The Ice and other stories

# The Pearl

**I**

**The first thing I remember – being on my father's shoulders.**
It's a winter night, there's a frost of stars in the sky, and my
breath clouds the air. It's my first memory of being alive, the
first thing in the world. We're there together at the bottom of
the garden, looking over the river, looking at the bridge. What
do I think it is? How does my two year old mind understand
it? This jewelled thing striding across the River Tay at its widest?
I don't understand it, but I see it all the same, and I see my
father pointing too, pointing at the train that's starting to cross.

Underneath the bridge it's silver, there's a sheen of
moonlight on this white-clear night, and the stars are crackling
and firing like gems above our house. For there are no
streetlights here; we're miles from the main road, miles from
Dundee, at the very edge of the river.

The train begins to cross and I watch it, enthralled. It's like a golden caterpillar, every window lit, and I can hear the roar of it as it begins the journey over. My father's babbling at me all the time, babbling and pointing, even though I can't understand a word he says. And I feel excited, even though I don't understand why. The world is exciting, is full of shining, precious things.

## II

The river has never stopped talking since the world began. Not a single time has it stopped running. In the beginning it's nothing, a thing so narrow it doesn't matter. Full of the silt of the hills. It's shallow, so thin a child could splash across. But it's the beginning just the same. It searches soft and untroubled under the Chinese Bridge, curls and curls again through pinewoods and lime-green glades. Until it meets the Lyon, grows stronger, pushes into the valley and is an arm that's clenched and ready.

The river has found its voice now. A boy can lie awake on a summer evening, not another sound in the world, and hold his breath to hear the silvering of the river through the blue night. It has breathed under the bridge and circled the town; now its swirls on over a wide beach of shingle and is gone. It reaches the rapids and becomes something on horseback, bucking and frothing among real rocks. Then, at a place of glades and bright flashes of kingfisher, it joins the Tummel.

This is where they come through the summer to stand in pools black as smoky quartz to play the water for salmon. It's a rushing now, straighter and more serious, a creature like several hundred greyhounds chasing to the sea. It can hear the sea, it's eager for the sea.

At last it comes down to Dunkeld, through woods planted by the old Dukes. The river swings round from south to east, passes the ancient walls of the cathedral built forgotten centuries ago by Celtic monks. They believed that places where rivers met were holy; that's why they chose these banks, for they lie directly opposite the narrow chattering of the Braan, the burn that has bounced out of the hills, brown and peaty and freezing cold.

But the journey's not over yet. The country's changing; the high ramparts of the hills are fading, folding into wide fields. This is where Georgina Ballantine pulled the biggest salmon ever recorded from a British river back in the reign of Queen Victoria.

So the river splits the city of Perth, passes under its bridges and is gone. Now the water is tidal, able to carry small ships back and forth to Dundee. The river is almost salty, scenting its own end. The banks are loud with the wrangling of geese and waterfowl; herons are posted in the shallows like sad old men in tattered overcoats. The river is so wide that on October days when the fog comes swirling in like clouds of candyfloss, you can't see the southern shore at all. Now the river slides under the railway bridge, and over there to the left is Dundee. The open coast's ahead – the sweet water's turned to sea.

## III

The pew is hard, my bottom sore. Sunlight blesses the church and I wish I was outside. I wish I could be going for chestnuts.

'Dearly beloved, how is a pearl made? It is one of the great miracles of God's world. A speck of dust, nothing more than a speck of dust, finds its way into the shell and is caught there. The shell knows it is there, it senses this scratch in itself, and swirls more of this beautiful white and shining skin to bury the intruder. It spins and spins, day after day and week after week, until it has made a pearl. A pearl is one of the finest creations there is, and yet at its heart – in its very core – there is a flaw.'

I want to shout out: 'My father's a pearlfisher!' But at that very moment I feel the pressure of his hand and look at him; there's the ghost of a smile on his lips and I want to know what he's thinking.

'That is the nature of this world of ours. Everything in it is fallen, everything is flawed. The pearl may look beautiful, may appear perfect, but its heart is dark and deceitful. That, my dear friends, is the state of humanity. No matter how good we may look on the surface, there is a fatal flaw in each one of us. No matter how much we spin white robes for ourselves, God can see the speck of sin at the heart of our lives.'

I watch a butterfly up against one of the stained glass windows. It's like a dry leaf, fluttering against the glass to get out. I glance at my dad and see that he's watching it too. The last butterfly of summer. I want to let it out, to free it, to watch it rise into the morning wind, but I know I have to sit there until the service is over. It's trapped and I want to help it but I can't. I feel the tears at the back of my eyes, burning and fierce. The minister's words all blur into one another so they become just a rising and falling in my head. All that matters in the world is the butterfly. I see its open wings and the perfect patterning of the panes on each one. Is there a speck of dust at its heart that made it? Is that why it's being punished now?

**IV**

Every Friday we went from our cottage at Fordie to her grave in that churchyard in Dundee, and every time it seemed to be raining. The road slushed with puddles as we hummed round bend after bend in that battered blue van, the smoke from my father's cigarette a sweet sourness in the air, the flowers on my knee somehow fading already. Every Friday evening we drove the five back road miles into Dundee and went first to Morganti's, where the yellow light hissed with bubbling cauldrons of chips, and a man who was no taller than me raked golden hills of fish. I crackled the last bits against my teeth as we sat in the warmth of the van. Then we had to go.

Even then it felt wrong that she was there, trapped in the middle of those concrete high rises, circled by loud roads. Even then, when I was seven or eight, it felt strange – though I wouldn't have known the words to say why.

KATHLEEN BORROW

The flowers glistened. I tried to gather the little bits of things I remembered of her as we crouched there; I tried to pick them like sprigs for a bouquet for the heart. She had died when I was four. I remembered a hillside and a kite, and I thought I could hear her voice. It was like hearing someone down below in an old house; the words were muffled and indistinct but the voice itself was familiar.

I could remember her singing, but not the place where she had sung. I could remember her hand, but not why she was holding mine. When I crouched there I didn't cry, I just hurt. It was as though someone had taken an implement and scraped out everything inside; I felt raw and sore and empty. My father smoked a cigarette and had it in his mouth the whole time; he moved twigs and scuffed away leaves and muttered at things and was never still, he was always moving.

I wanted to know what had happened, why she had died. But I had grown away from the little sprigs of things I remembered of her; they were stories I told myself when we went to her grave on a Friday. They were stories I told myself after he had been angry with me and I lay curled into myself in bed, my face still wet with crying. But the hand that had held my own was cold, the voice that had sung was strange.

I felt raw and sore and empty, but also because of that place and the rain, the high rises and the grey skies. Yet the longer that passed, the more I wanted to know what had killed my mother. And the harder it was to ask.

# V

A year after my father was incarcerated in a locked ward I dared to go and visit Sandy MacPhee. A place on the old Drummond estate, up an abomination of a track that the car whined and sputtered its way. Spring and daffodils were Easter trumpets in the fields; odd scars of snow still grey in the high hills and a wind that cut like a knife.

I got out and was up to my ankles in mud. I swore and thudded the car door shut, tucking the glugging bottle under my coat, and swam the last yards to the house. It was no house now, it was the remains of what once had been a house. The walls thumped and shook with dogs as I hammered at the door. This was a mistake, this was stupid beyond words.

Nothing. I felt almost relieved. I could go, I could get out. Then something inside; the remains of a voice gathering itself – coughing, a cough that tore up the lungs. The sound of feet moving and searching, a voice cursing.

The door opened a few inches. That face with its burst rivers of capillaries, a pulp of redness, and its wet eyes.

He knew who I was. He didn't have to ask.

'Did I bother to get up for you? Come in, damn it, and leave the cold behind you. Lie down, Hamish! Meg, get out of it! Clear a space for yourself, man. I'm not going to do it for you. I'm held together by string and whisky!'

He collapsed back on a sofa from which he'd swept three empty cans with the back of one hand. I tried to breathe through my mouth; there was dog mess wet in the corner of the room. One of the whippets had come back and was padding about, licking something from the floor. Sandy lit a cigarette and another wave of coughing came over him; he was nothing more than a house of sticks – those were the words that came to me. His eyes bled tears.

'So why are you here?' he asked, once he'd recovered something of his voice. He looked at me from that sofa and it was hard to look back at him. He was like something that had been squashed on a road, that should be put out of its misery.

'Are you a doctor or a lawyer or what? Have you come to turf me out?'

I put the whisky on the table and his eyes followed it. That was an answer too.

'I've come to find my father, Sandy.'

He whipped his head under the sofa. 'Don't see him there, do you?'

I gave him the smile he wanted. 'No, I know where he is. Up in that white elephant of a hospital, being pumped full of twenty drugs a day. He doesn't know his own name. There's so much I don't know. You know more than I do.'

He looked at me and his eyes, those wet eyes, were filled with many things. He just kept watching me from where he lay on that filthy sofa, then dragged himself up. He looked so frail I thought he might snap, yet I reckon he was strong still. He was all wire.

'There's things I can tell you and things I can't.'

I didn't answer that. I didn't rise to the bait. I was waiting.

'Your father was a good man, Neil. He was a good man. We understood each other. We weren't always friends, but we understood each other. He came up from England sometime in the 1960s – don't ask me what it was that brought him. He never talked about that, not a word. But the Borrows were travellers all right, English travellers. If he hadn't had traveller blood I wouldn't have taught him what I did, taught him pearlfishing. Everything I bloody knew. Three summers we fished the rivers together and we got good pearls, we got good prices. We camped out for weeks on end and were brown as nuts the two of us.'

He was flowing now, he was like his own river. This was what I wanted, this was what I had yearned. But then he stopped; it was as though he came to, woke up, heard himself. The eyes were wet with venom again; the gift of the whisky was forgotten.

'What happened then?' I asked, leaning forwards in the chair.

'You know damn well what happened then!' he spat, and his voice broke into a cackle, a tearing of coughing that might have brought the walls down. He looked at me like a drowning man, but he didn't want help. He didn't want rescued.

'After that we couldn't talk again,' he whispered. 'It would have been more than my life was worth.' And he turned away on the sofa, he turned away.

## VI

It was that same night it happened. The geese were leaving, going back to Iceland; the fields around Dundee were loud with their wrangling and their long trails of skeins were like threads in the skies to the north. They were winter blue those skies; what I once called *faraway blue*. My father had liked that – it had pleased him and he had laughed as we went back along the farm track home, our feet squelching in

September mud. He said the words to himself and laughed, and I felt a dizzy warmth that went all through me. I had pleased my father; I had said something that pleased him.

I felt filthy after visiting Sandy MacPhee's. I stood under the shower a full half hour, washing that place from my skin, scrubbing it away. But it wasn't just the place. It was much more than that I was washing away, and when I came out at last – a single, thin, white shiver of bone – I wasn't sure if I was any cleaner at all. I crept into bed and wrapped the sheet round me, shivering. I heard a train rattling and squealing over the Tay and I remembered it from the bedroom window, from the cottage I'd grown in, and I remembered being on my father's shoulders to watch it. Was it one memory, or was it hundreds that had crashed together in the dark of my mind like railway carriages, fused into one?

I must have slept, through it was a shallow sleep, like blue water. I remember waking somewhere in the middle of the night, hearing something I couldn't recognise at first. I rose out of the shallow water and turned, lifted my head, held my breath. Then it came again, a single pipe in the dark, a cry. I knew what it was before I could name it; the sound made sense before I caught it. A goose, one single goose. And then it came to me that the travellers believed that if you heard a single goose flying round the house at night it meant you would go on a journey. I sat up and listened, and there was just the slightest edge of grey in the room. It must have been very early morning; the goose was lost in the fog.

It was as though I was hauled back into my four year old skin. I heard my father's steps clumping at the cottage door, and I knew it was him at once. I had been waiting for him for nine whole days and he was home! I heard my mother's soft voice welcoming him, smoothing him, and I wanted to run downstairs and see him – I wanted to so badly. But I was supposed to be asleep and my mother might be angry. I got up all the same and padded over the floor to the window; I curled the curtain back and saw the van in the yard, and the pale lantern of the moon riding the summer skies. I could hear the soft thatch of early morning birdsong in the trees.

He came inside and the door closed. I heard their soft steps on the stairs, the close murmur of their voices. My father sounded excited and I wanted to hear the words, I wanted to know what he was saying. I leant my ear hard against the cold wall, held my breath.

'I've never seen the river so low, Kathleen, it was hardly higher than my knees. Not a soul about, five o'clock in the morning, nothing but me and a cloud of midges. So I go up, right, the whole hundred yards in the water – the place that Sandy took me last year. Nearly broke my bloody ankle, the stones were that slippy! There's this pool, right, black as death – even at the height of summer it's five feet deep. So I get the crook, put it right down – slow, slow. I use my glass and I pull up mussel after mussel. Thing is I didn't expect a damn thing! It's a place the tinkers know, they've been guarding it since the Flood! Then I pull up something else; I can feel it's different even before I see it. This huge shell all bent and lop-sided, and I can tell it's special from the outside – I just know! I was shaking, I was shaking that bad I thought I wouldn't make it out again. I don't know how I made it yet. I sat on that bank and just held it, Kathleen. It was like a gift, something nobody else knew about, not even the tinkers. This was one they'd missed. Then I opened it. I got out my knife and opened it. I slipped away the flesh inside and could feel it even then, but I didn't look. Then it was there, Kathleen.'

I forgot myself, burst open the door and went out across the corridor into their room. I caught their faces, the two white ovals. But my father's hand was still open, bent low. And there in the middle of it was a great, perfect, pure, shining pearl. The biggest there had ever been. . .

•

1976. The year my mother died, and the year my father found the pearl. Had I really forgotten, or had I shoved the memory into the dark attics of my head and locked it away to die? It was Sandy MacPhee who had brought it back, Sandy had dug up the key. I lay there, breathing hard, as if I had run through a deep forest. I felt different just the same; I felt a curious sense of well-being. The goose had gone; the goose had found its way after all.

Then the phone rang. Out in the hall the phone began ringing. It was five past five. Nothing in the world is worse than a telephone ringing in the night; every fear there is shrieks from that shrill ringing, from that black cradle. I blundered out into the hall and stared at it. It rang and rang and I did not go nearer, I did not leave it; I just stared, hearing my own heart. Then I reached out, white, through the darkness, lifted it to my ear.

'Hello?'

'Mr Borrow? Neil Borrow? I'm so sorry to disturb you this early in the morning, but it's your father. He's disappeared.

He must have managed to get out one of the windows on an upper floor, sometime very late last night. We need your help to find him.'

**VII**

So he went to Perth with the pearl, in the summer of 1976. That summer when the rivers were thirsty with drought, little more than blue ribbons dribbling over stones. The hills were arid things, staring out into still blue skies, day after dizzy day. That was how he found it to begin with, the pearl – because it had been so deep in its pool it had never been seen by the travellers. But it was his now, this thing as big as his pinkie nail – perfect, the most perfect pearl the river had known in all the long journey of its life.

He went to Perth, to that place that was once the capital of Scotland, the place of kings. A shadow of itself now, nothing more than a slump on the banks of the river; a place that hated itself. Out on the edges, up in the green and sleepy fringes, grey villas half-asleep whose woods were loud with the cawing of crows. The homes of tweedy men with light blonde wives who held the strings of the city and knew it. But in the dead centre of it all, in the narrow vennels and back streets, people who might almost have been fathered by this sick city itself, who limped and had disfigured faces, who were crippled by drink, whose minds were missing things.

This is where my father came, upriver from Dundee, when I was four, with one pearl in his pocket. Because this is where they came from all over the Highlands, the travellers, to the jewellers whose name was known everywhere from Dunkeld to Durness, to those who could write it and to those whose tongue alone could speak it – *Cairncross*. There in the heart of Perth, one street behind the City Hall, the place that bought pearls.

He would have gone there from Fordie in his best clothes, my mother would have made sure of that. And I know even his hand trembled as he opened the fine glass door that brilliant blue morning and was back there in the world that belonged to Cairncross. For he had been there before, perhaps first with Sandy, with grey-rimmed pearls from the Lyon one day, and rose-edged pearls from the Esk another. But that day he went alone, his hands trembling, with the biggest pearl they would ever see.

They ushered him through to the backshop, their voices soft before they had even an inkling as to what he brought with him. For the same courtesy was shown to prince and peasant, and that was how it had always been. They wore black suits and white gloves, and you were offered a chair before another word was said. And then my father would have smiled – I can see him now, with that boyish grin that first won my mother – as he opened the shell of his hand to let the pearl into the light.

**VIII**

So I went looking for him that day, looking for a man who was lost, who had managed to find the one window in all that faceless whiteness that wasn't locked, and escape.

They had sent him there because they didn't know what else to do with him, because there was no book on their

The Ice and other stories

shelves that told them how to heal a man who was broken inside and bleeding from a wound they could neither see nor reach. He drank because he felt guilt for what he'd done, and for what he hadn't. He was trying to wash away a scar inside.

There were so many questions I wanted answered, but when I went to visit him and the key was turned behind me on that locked ward, I knew he was the last person to ask. There was nothing there in that puffed face on the pillows or inside the blue eyes that stared at me, glazed and foolish with their crazy concoction of pills. I was beside the man who used to be my father.

I drove all day, following the course of the river, but I'm not sure if I was looking for him or not. Perhaps I was just looking for myself. I went up into Glen Lyon, the longest glen in Scotland, at whose heart is the River Lyon – a creature made of polished, black, smoky quartz. The road is a confusion of bends and passing places twenty-six miles long. Somehow it's never the same; whenever I go back there are places that startle me, distances that confound me. It's a place full of strangeness and stories old as the rocks themselves.

It was early evening when the car shuddered to a standstill and I thudded the door shut, went down under the beech trees to a long edge of gravel and grey stones. The river was fierce, fleeced with melted snow and freezing. I bent down and cupped a deep handful, and my fingers hurt with that cold. The soreness of that water echoed and echoed inside.

I crouched there, looking upstream and thinking, watching the fierce roar of the Lyon as it rocked towards me, loud with April. And I remembered something else; this thing dislodged from the back of my mind and was washed out into that moment – undamaged and intact.

I was lying in my room in the cottage and I was afraid. I didn't know why I was afraid but I knew without any doubt that I was. I was afraid and I was listening and it was the middle of the night. I listened and I heard a noise, almost like that of a creature, a creature in agony, in slow and terrible pain. And behind it was another noise, a rushing loudness, a great breaking of water that went on and on and on. And the first sound was my father's weeping, tearing itself apart, and the second the autumn spate of the river – the Tay raging its last miles to the sea. I lay there not moving, never having heard my father cry before. I was four years old and my mother was dead.

## IX

Three weeks and no word of him. A helicopter fluttered over the low country and the pantiled hamlets behind Dundee like a blue dragonfly, there was an article in the paper and a picture of the way he was – the pearlfisher. They found the black and white one too, showing the great pearl, and of course the story had to be told again. Then they forgot. There were mud slides in Mexico and bomb alerts in Beirut, and the story of an old man who'd escaped from a mental home wasn't exciting any longer. And the river turned beautiful and blue; the oystercatchers piped like bands of children on holiday from school, and I was empty-handed. I did not know where to look. I did not know where to find my father because I did not know him. And so one Saturday I went back to Sandy MacPhee.

I woke up that morning with an urgency that trembled in my hands. What if the traveller was dead already? What if my father was dead? It was that lost time, between the finding of the great pearl and my mother's death – that was what made no sense, that was the lost time.

The track on the Drummond estate was rutted and baked like clay – there'd been no real rain for days now. One of the estate workers was labouring up its steepness; as the car whined towards him he stopped, turned and looked – eyes dark and full of questions, hands buried deep in khaki pockets.

'I'm going to see Sandy MacPhee,' I told him as I drew level with him. I nearly told him whose son I was, then I stopped myself. 'How is he?'

The shoulders shrugged almost imperceptibly, the dark eyes ran over my car and me. But my passport had been accepted all the same. My father had known these estates so well; little feudal principalities where the pheasant was God. For eleven months of the year the birds were worshipped and adored; in the twelfth they were blasted out of the skies.

'MacPhee? How should I know?' Reproach and resentment. 'You can remind him to pay his rent when you see him.'

I'd already wound up the window and looked away. I was already driving on, an old anger rising in me dark as bile. I remembered the man who came to our cottage, to Fordie, in the years after my mother was dead. The hammer at the door that could be no-one else's, that said everything in its curt violence. I remembered the fear that rose like black wings in my chest, that made me run away and stand at the back of the house, watching and fearing that this time we'd be evicted. Because I knew that word – it was one of the first words I learned. I remembered my father staggering out, swearing, half-gone with drink but well enough able to pull himself tall to stand with fierce dignity before that Barbour-clad factor not half his age. It was a chess game of power where you were always and only a pawn; where the other side had all the knights and the bishops, the kings and the queens – where all you could do was lose.

I was going to knock at Sandy's door, but then I remembered something and hesitated. I called his name instead, questioning, and listened. Nothing, not even dogs. I looked round and the edge of the wood bloomed with sunlight. I had no choice. I opened the door.

He was lying there on that couch, all that was left of him, as if he'd never got up again after I left him at Easter. There was just less of him, that was all. I sat down opposite him, leant forwards.

'Sandy?'

He fought with his eyes, something in his throat struggled.

'Sandy, it's Neil Borrow.' I paused. 'John's son. Can I get you something?'

He opened his eyes and they searched, wet and blue and big. I remembered him coming once to Fordie, jigging me onto his shoulder and taking me down to the river, he and my father bright with laughter, cigarettes in their mouths.

I answered my own question, got up and found a cup, filled it from a dripping tap. I made him drink, had to support it for him.

'Sandy.' He wanted to sleep and I wouldn't let him. I needed him before it was too late. 'Sandy, I want to know what happened to my father afterwards, after he found the pearl.' It was too sudden, too much, but I felt time slipping through my hands like water.

He looked at me, the lost islands of his eyes moving and drifting. I took the cup away and pulled the filthy pillow higher under his head – bringing him back, dragging him back. Then suddenly he did rouse, he moved on the couch and seemed to climb higher into himself again.

'It finished him.' The words set fire to his chest; he tried to sit up as the coughing rattled his frame. He spat brown into his hand. But the eyes swam back to me all the same. 'No-one would speak to him. The travellers hated him. He'd beaten us, damn it. Beaten us at our own game. He was rich and what good did it do him? He was famous, but it gave him nothing. Nothing. And he'd sold the story. Every river in Scotland was being raped for pearls. People who didn't know a pearl from a potato. They raped the rivers. And it was his fault. He knew it. And he'd sold it. He didn't even have the pearl.' His voice was scarcely more than a whisper, a breath. 'That's what happened.'

I nodded, my hands held together as I leaned over close to him. That was it, that was what had happened. He'd given me my answer. He was finished.

Suddenly I thought of something, something that had been at the back of my mind since I came.

'The dogs, Sandy. What about your dogs?'

The eyes softened, blinked. 'Took them away,' he whispered.

'Who took them away? Who did that?'

But he was retreating into himself, he was disappearing. He'd given as much as he wanted and now he didn't want to any longer. It wasn't only that he couldn't. He was a traveller; to the last he was a traveller. I had known what that meant all my life, since I shared a classroom with them from the age of five. They were different; they shared the same roads I walked, they knew the same names for the same hills and the same rivers – yet they were different. They were themselves.

'Sandy.' He was almost away, almost gone. I had felt sorry for him, and that was the last thing in the world he would have wanted. There was defiance in those eyes; they would be defiant when they came to carry him out dead.

'Sandy, d'you know where my father is?' Helpless; me the supplicant, leaning forwards, pleading for answers. This wreck of humanity curled into himself, all of five stone, his eyes scornful.

Did I really not know? Had I not worked it out? All that I heard in the one word he gave me:

'Fordie.'


## X


I can remember wishing when I was a boy that there was a machine for listening to voices. I mean voices from the past. You had to imagine walls being like tree trunks, with rings of time inside them; the machine would go deeper and deeper into sound time until it could go no further. I wanted it then because I knew my mother's voice was in the walls; it was lying asleep in them and the machine could bring the words back and play them. I could hear her voice again.

I remembered that as I drove down the estate road, through the harp strings of that sharp Spring light, and I wasn't sure I would want it now. I had prayed then that the machine I dreamed of might be invented so I could hear my mother's voice, but it was everything else it would bring that I feared.

In that tree there was the memory of me crying, crying because no-one loved me and I loved no-one. In that wall was the memory of the twisted words that came from my father's mouth when he fell there and shattered his jaw, his head wretched with drink. There were little hints of light too, of the friends I had found at last who turned in the wood and smiled at me, of bristling red squirrels in the pines I spent hours watching – but it was the dark that came at me as I drove. It came from every side with its voices, its whispers, and enveloped me. I wanted to go back and yet I didn't. I'm not sure if I lacked courage, or if I was brave for the first time in my life.

The cottage was empty. Fordie, the place I'd spent more years of my life than anywhere else. Strange I knew it was empty; something about the glazed panes of the windows, like eyes with cataracts. So much smaller than I remembered. The duck egg blue of the walls and the white frames of the windows just the same. I tried the door and went inside, just a step, and listened. All of my senses listened, there in the damp darkness. At my feet were two dead matches, still crisp.

I turned involuntarily and saw him, even then. Down by the river, beside the pool. I started over, dizzy, and he didn't look in my direction, even though I knew he knew I was there.

'Where have you been?' A plea, an accusation, a question – awe, bewilderment, admiration.

Now he looked up, so different, older and yet the same. The puffed, foolish face gone; the bloated hands flabby with their cocktails of drugs washed clean and thin. A river had coursed through him, had swept away the white emptiness of that place that had clogged him, that had numbed him and left him a dunce. His eyes were his own, they danced with their own river – with precious, shining things. And then I knew too that he hadn't drunk anything, that the whisky he drank to forget, to forget to remember, was gone. He was clean. He looked at me from where he sat by the river and was clear and white. He was himself.

'I've been here.' He said it as if it was the most natural thing in the world, and the torrent of questions that came to me dried in my mouth. Something in him had been alive just the same in that place, something in him that yearned to be free, that had to escape, go back. He had returned to the river; it was as though like a salmon he had heard it, felt its tug, had had to find it.

I went closer and crouched down opposite him, hands in my coat. He looked at me all the time. He had not held my gaze like that for more years than I could remember. He was good at looking away, at getting on with something else, at escaping. I felt a flash of anger through me like lightning. I had looked up to him; how I had looked up to the pearlfisher who had found the great pearl, how I had bragged about him and defended him. Yet how he had squandered that. I loved him and I hated him for it.

I wanted to tell him they had been searching, we had all been searching, that there had been helicopters and boats and a hundred people scouring the country. I wanted to tell him. . . But all of it fell away, all of it washed away and was useless, and instead there was burning in my eyes and the

The Ice and other stories

tears ran hot down my face, as he held my gaze and would not look away. There was nothing in all the world I could do but cry.

He had scolded me so often for crying; there was nothing enraged him so much in those years as my crying. He would rampage about the cottage, banging doors and doing things and shouting, beside himself with rage and frustration. Now he only looked at me; he would not look away. In all those years, since I was four, he had not looked at me, he had not held my gaze. Now I wanted him to look away and he would not.

'I came here because I had to. This is the place I had to face. I had to come here before it was too late, and I felt it here, I knew it.'

I looked at him through the glassy mess of my crying. I watched him as he watched me; I couldn't look away. But my eyes were asking him too, were searching and questioning. For a second he did look away, down at the water, at the pool. For a second he flinched.

'Your mother,' he said. 'This is where your mother. . . The year I found the pearl, the year I found that damned pearl and you were four. I didn't know what to do with myself, Neil, I didn't know what to do. I was so full of anger, so full of anger all the time. She tried, she tried to find me, time after time after time.' He hugged himself as though the soreness was bad, as if a hook pulled through him. 'One night she couldn't any more. She came out here and went into the river. That's why I was the way I was for all those years. Because I knew it was my fault, because I couldn't go back. All because of the pearl.'

And I understood at last. I nodded and held his gaze, across the water of the pool, as a train began its rattle across the bridge, made of golden light.

# Billy

**It was my mother's fault. I was fifteen years old and evidently** doing too little on Saturdays. I appeared, very scrubbed, at the counter of Billy Bride's shop Food for Thought, just before closing time on Halloween.

'So you can do Saturdays. Nine to half five. No coming in at quarter to ten in your pyjamas – isn't that right, Fran?'

His wife, small and dark, appeared from the back shop and her eyes glinted at his wink. I kept my hands rigidly by my sides.

'What team d'you support?'

I swallowed. I wondered if this was a trick question, a part of the interview. I really wasn't all that bothered about football; my allegiance was tacit, something to trot out on occasions when I simply had to – like now:

'Celtic.'

Billy let out a string of words that would have turned the

apples behind me sour. My cheeks burned.

'Should we let him work here, Fran?' he said, turning to face her. 'I don't think a Celtic supporter should get their fingers within half a mile of my till!' He looked at me, his eyes suddenly softer. 'See you nine o'clock Saturday.'

•

Billy sold everything, everything edible that is. Cartloads of potatoes, fields of vegetables, enough cheese to satisfy the mice of Wolverhampton for a week. It was a strange old warren of a place with stone floors; there was a yard at the back for the lorries to off-load their sacks and boxes, a cooler ten feet deep, and back rooms filled with weighing machines and tables. And there was a room that was Billy's, an office with a telephone and a desk and a radio.

'And how's my favourite girl today? A quarter of Parma ham? Now, you were asking about honey last week, Mrs Armstrong. Fran, did we not get honey from the market last Sunday?'

I came and went with oranges and halves of cucumber for the stands. In the back shop I weighed out potatoes in four and seven pound bags, and staggered along the road to distant cars with full sacks. I answered the telephone, and with a trembling pen took down orders from nearby estates for shooting parties, and from elderly ladies who always had their groceries very kindly delivered by Mr and Mrs Bride.

But at ten to three Billy disappeared into the office and shut the door. I looked questioningly at Fran.

'The Match,' she said.

The Ice and other stories

At five to three she went in with a cup of tea and a bar of chocolate. I heard the roars from the crowd at Ibrox; the Rangers' fans were in good voice.

At half past, when I was putting out fresh pears, a Mrs Porter came into the shop. She smiled and asked if she might have a word with Billy.

'I'm terribly sorry, but he's down in Glasgow today looking at melons.' That was the message I'd been told to convey. I felt my cheeks going pink. A disappointed Mrs Porter thanked me and was gone.

At twenty past four Fran and I jumped as a fist hammered the office table. The radio was clicked off. There wasn't a sound from the place for another hour; the office lay dark and still.

We fluttered here and there like butterflies – serving customers and carrying boxes. Once I dared to glance in as I passed on my way to the back shop for potatoes. He was sunk over the desk as if he'd been punctured by a pin.

At five to five Fran crumpled a ten pound note into my hand and fitted a bag of over-ripe plums under my arm.

'He'll be fine tomorrow,' she breathed, as if he had a touch of 'flu. 'We'll see you next Saturday.'

•

So that was how the winter went. I spent my Saturdays at Food for Thought, and began to save a fair amount of money from my time there. Occasionally Billy would phone and ask if I could come in early at six to help unload some sacks from a supplier, and I think I always said yes. It wasn't just because my mother would have been most displeased if I'd said that I couldn't, that wasn't the only reason. And I was the last one to like getting up early on a Saturday morning.

I can remember going down to the place at ten to six. The town was dead, not a light showing. And the darkness was blue, not black – it was a really dark blue. I had my hands dug as deep into my pockets as they'd go, as the leaves gusted about the pavements in a wind that might have been coming straight from Murmansk.

It wasn't that I liked doing those sacks. Billy once described me as built for pushing envelopes rather than heavy weights, and that was pretty near the mark. Angus, the lorry driver, gave me a toothless grin and didn't need to utter the words he was thinking so loudly.

I remember once counting thirty-nine sacks. By then I felt as if my life was over; even walking was a penance. But we went into the office, Billy's den, and the gas fire was lit so it grew hot and orange and hissing, and there was tea and a bar of chocolate.

•

And Billy and I talked. It wasn't about big things, about the state of the world or the health service, or what I was going to do with my life. We talked about the town, about Mrs Richardson who'd had six children, about George Galbraith who was tipped to play football for Scotland, about the big, new supermarket that was opening next year and was going to kill the place.

But mostly Billy and I talked football (or, more accurately, Billy talked and I listened). What Billy didn't know about football wasn't worth knowing. He knew why it was a certain team had won a cup; how it was that that particular goalkeeper had ended up playing for a certain side. He knew why matches had been cancelled and what had happened to particular players when they retired. Billy didn't just know the statistics, the dull lists to be found in dusty books on library shelves – Billy knew the stories behind them, and he told them with a burning eagerness, an excitement that set them alight. When Fran came in to get the shop ready for opening at ten to nine I was far away. I'd been taken on amazing journeys.

Then, when Hogmanay had come and gone, the day of the traditional Old Firm match between Celtic and Rangers dawned, and Billy was ready. There were two tins of beer on the office table for a win, one tin for a draw, and neither Fran nor myself dared tempt fate by asking what would happen in the event of a defeat. The radio went on at half past two; the first cup of tea and bar of chocolate went into the office at quarter to the hour. Now all we could do was wait.

The roars from Ibrox were loud enough to be heard in the shop. So were the roars from Billy. It would be no earthly good telling people he was anywhere but the office. And if they wanted to disturb him, it was at their own peril. . .

At half-time he appeared himself and began breezing about the back place in a very agitated state, a cigarette between his lips. I dared to go through cautiously for some seven pound bags of potatoes. He was staring out into empty space.

'1 – 0 down,' he murmured. 'And a player sent off in the thirty-eighth minute.'

I relayed the news to Fran. She nodded, pale, and ten minutes after the second half had begun and the chanting was well underway, she went in with a second cup of tea. But she was blown out like a breeze, and the door banged behind her.

•

The seconds ticked by. Mrs Armitage came in to pick up a delivery for the Lodge, and had a long and delicate conversation with Fran about the consistency and overall quality of the shop's Brie. Some elderly ladies, obviously from a bus party, came in to shelter from the rain, squeezed one or two pears and wandered round commenting on local prices. They took wing like three startled pigeons when a string of expletives came from the office and something was thumped. After that the delivery lorry from the creamery arrived and to my relief I was able to go and busy myself with trays of yoghurt. It was just beginning to get dark.

At ten to five the office door suddenly flew open. Billy came out, his face blotchy with rage, his beloved blue and white socks dangling from his extended left hand like a bad smell. He barged his way past me onto the pavement, dropped his socks into the gutter, and lit them with his lighter. Fran and I glanced at each other, working out just how many goals must have gone against his beloved team in the end. I reckoned four or five. I should have been pleased; it was, after all, 'my' team that had won. I just felt numb, numb and queer in the stomach. I didn't know what to do next. Billy had burnt his Rangers socks.

All that January he didn't listen to the radio on Saturdays. He just sat in the office, hunched over the desk in the half-light of those grim winter afternoons. Fran didn't take him tea or chocolate, she just served the trickle of customers that came in, and told them Billy wasn't so well, that he'd be back in on Monday.

On the 7th of February, about half past nine that Friday evening, I phoned just to check there wasn't to be an early delivery the following morning. I was quite bushy-tailed; a girl called Moira whom I'd been adoring from afar for six long months had agreed to come to the cinema with me that Saturday night.

But Fran sounded far away at the end of the phone, it was as though the line between us stretched far further than to the end of the neighbouring village where they lived. She sounded small and muffled.

'Billy's dead,' she said.

I couldn't sleep that night. I lay on my back on the bed and didn't get undressed. The curtains were open and the light was off. My mother went to bed at eleven and called good night from along the corridor. I don't know if I answered or not. The wind came in big gusts and was loud in the trees; it banged over the dustbin and sent it rolling up and down the path. A branch tapped in Morse code against the window, and I understood every message it sent.

•

Then, at just after quarter past two in the morning, I got up. I went downstairs as though sleepwalking, my footsteps soft on the stairs. I clicked open the front door and started down the road, not even a jacket on my back. I had a key in my pocket; the key Billy and Fran had given me for emergencies.

I went inside and shivered. The cooler roared when I opened the door; the stacks of spring onions and radishes, the tomatoes and cauliflowers all in suspended animation, waiting. I padded round the grey bleakness of the shop, hearing the click of the clock and the scatterings of leaves as they rushed along the pavements, hurried away by the wind.

I went through to the back shop and looked at the shadows of the huge weighing machines, and somehow they were like people there on the tables, figures all hunched over. Then I went without a sound and stood, hearing nothing but my own breathing, at the door of Billy's office. I always knocked before going in, and I knocked again now.

I sat in the chair I'd always sat in, the one I took on delivery days when I was there from six in the morning. I put on the gas fire, all three bars, and waited for it to turn hot and orange. I heard the wind wild in the chimney, gusting down.

There on the table was a pack of Billy's cigarettes, right beside me. It was almost as though he'd left them like that deliberately, knowingly. I stared at the carton for a long time and then, very carefully, not moving the packet itself from the angle at which it lay, I opened it and took one out with trembling fingers.

That first drag of smoke made the world strange and dizzy. My head was spinning and I tried to focus on the orange dragon of the gas fire. Then everything steadied again and my hand stopped shaking. I wasn't sorry. It felt right, exactly what Billy would have wanted me to do. I sat there and smoked, and all his best stories of football chased through my mind – of infamous victories and unbearable defeats, of amazing triumphs snatched in the nick of time. I smoked that

The Ice and other stories

one cigarette and I cried. I sat in that chair, small and cold and fifteen years of age, and I cried for Billy who was gone and who would never come back again.

Then I closed the shop, slipped the key under the back door, and set off home. I didn't go to Billy's funeral, despite all my mother's protestations. I had double maths that afternoon and went off up Drummond Hill instead. I sat at the top and got my breath back, on a day when the lapwings were tumbling and crying in the fields, and the skies were torn between blue and grey. The last snow lay in pockets in the shadows of the hills; the new year was beginning, the Spring was coming back at last.

A football supporter? You're asking if I'm a football supporter? Didn't I tell you before? Oh, yes, I'm a fanatical Rangers fan.

# Cloudberries

**It was the first train in the morning from Oslo to Lillehammer.**
Solveig waited beside her mother and could hear the pattering
of her own heart. She could smell things on the platform: the
tobacco a young soldier was smoking, the perfume from her
mother's hand, and the cheese on her grandparents' farm.

She couldn't really smell that because she was not there
yet. But in two and half hours she would smell it again and
she would go with her grandfather to the milking sheds as
she always did on the first evening she arrived. Her mother
was telling her all the things she wasn't to do, but Solveig
swam in and out of listening as she might have swum through
pools of shallow water (she had learned to swim that year),
and as her mother was always telling her what she couldn't
do there was no real point listening. She was much too
concerned about the rust-red train that was sliding to a
standstill beside them, worried that she might not have a

window seat. She broke away from her mother's hand.

'Solveig!' Her mother's scolding was lost in the noise as folk clamoured to find their seats. It was the height of summer; families were flooding out of Oslo to the countryside and they hadn't a moment to lose.

'Find me a cloudberry,' her mother murmured through the window. Now Solveig smiled; her mouth puckered like a flower and the morning sunlight lemoned her cheek. She was saying yes.

Then the whistle was blown, the train started out of the station and Solveig watched as her mother became a toy person among a whole crowd of diminishing figures waving and calling out things that were soundless. She had found a seat by the window that let her travel backwards; that was how she liked to be in the train, watching things till they were swallowed in the past. The lady opposite her brought out a bag of sweets and offered her one; Solveig said thank you and then could say no more for the next five minutes as the mint-flavoured ball filled the whole of her mouth. She was going to her grandparents for the next two weeks and something like blue light filled her from top to bottom. Even if she had been able to speak with the sweet in her mouth she would have found no words. But she wondered to herself at that moment if looking forward was bigger than getting there, than being there. Was looking forward the most special thing there could be?

•

'You've put on weight!' said her grandfather when he caught

her as she jumped from the last step. She wanted to ask him a hundred and fifty questions about the farm, about the cats, about her cousins in the village, about the house (for the attic had been repaired since she was last there), but she didn't know which question should come first. She just looked at him with big eyes as he carried her bags, and he looked back at her and ruffled her hair.

That night she lay on her back and didn't want to sleep. In Oslo the traffic kept her awake at night. There she tried to bury her head in the pillow and escape into sleep; here she wanted to stay awake and found her eyes heavier with every second. It was still light and her grandparents were having supper down in the kitchen. She could hear the low murmur of the television as they watched the news. Her grandmother had baked fresh rolls; she'd made the first pots of wild raspberry jam. Her grandfather was drinking his last cup of strong coffee of the day. She could hear the tinkling of the sheep bells outside; her window was open to let in the summer air and she could hear the rush of the wind in the woods like a strange sea. She was washed away on its tide and into the morning.

She made a den up on the edge of the wood and kept her diary there. She and her boy cousins made dams on the river; they played there until eight in the evening and her grandmother had to come and find her. She caught her first fish and met a boy called Dag Karsten whose hair was so fair it was like ripe wheat. She wanted to run her hand through it but she couldn't and when she looked at him she felt strange, as she'd never felt before in her life. And the days ran like warm sand between her hands.

It was the third last night and she'd had supper. Normally she was chased off upstairs as soon as the news came on, but not tonight. The skies were a kind of green-blue; the sun had gone down but a weird luminous glow remained. There wasn't a breath of wind and the sheep made not a sound; they were lying in the field on the edge of the forest, white ridges of sheep.

Solveig sat by the kitchen window and watched the skies. It was as if something new and wonderful was about to happen, and then as she watched, it did. A great white ghost of moon floated up from behind the hills like a balloon, like a balloon wobbling with water, and it rose grazed and scuffed and ancient, and lay huge and beautiful in the August skies.

•

Her grandmother slipped the handle of a small pail over her right hand. She looked round, bewildered.

'Cloudberries,' she said softly. 'We're going to pick cloud-berries, up on the edge of the moor.'

She put on her outdoor shoes and a fleece; her grand-mother smeared her face and neck with a cream against mosquitoes.

'Why doesn't grandpa get any?' Solveig asked, her face a crinkled mask of disgust.

'Because I'm used to them,' he said, and she could hear the smile in his voice.

Then they had left the back door and were walking like snails through the long grass in the field. That was how she thought of it, for snails left a trail behind them and so did they. When she looked round there were three weaving trails in the long grass. She wanted to sing but she listened and realised it was so quiet she couldn't. It would have been wrong; the moon and the green-blue skies and the quiet were too special. She listened instead, to their feet in the grass – their soft feet in the grass.

The insects came round their faces and heads in a grey dancing. Sometimes they tickled her cheeks but they didn't bite. The pails swished against their sides as they began to climb the hill path.

Cloudberries. Mountain brambles; beaded berries that turned red first and then honey-orange. They melted on the tongue and they were ready, now, in August. Sometimes Solveig thought that finding them was the biggest thing in the year, bigger even than Christmas or her own birthday. Knowing that the cloudberries were ready and going to find them!

They came up onto the moorland and the mountains beyond were like blue whales lying on their backs. Up above the white lantern of the moon gave the land a strange glow. Solveig could have walked and walked all night and never missed her footing. It was like a painting she had seen in the National Gallery in Oslo; she stopped and watched, her face filled with light.

Then she began running. She had a promise to keep.

# The Sledge

'You're not going anywhere without breakfast, Samuel Carter!'

He hunched over the porridge, submissive and reluctant.

'Alan Benson doesn't have to eat porridge in the morning, nor Clare Sidbury!'

His mother came clumping though from the kitchen and her blue eyes flashed at him.

'Well, I don't say much for their chances in life, that's all I can say. The British Empire was built on porridge and don't you forget it!'

The back door rasped open and his father appeared in the frame of it – big, beetroot-cheeked, breath streaming from his mouth in great dragons, and snowflakes twirling behind him, big as cats' paws.

'No good. The car's in the garage for the next fortnight. And there isn't a road for it to go on anyway – it's eight inches deep in snow and there's another bundle of the stuff coming.'

His mother turned the dial of the wireless through hissing, a bit of Brahms, distant German, and someone singing – to the sudden clear English steadiness of the BBC. '. . . parts of the country are so badly affected that all the but the more major routes are closed. In rural Buckinghamshire, two schoolchildren had a narrow escape when a quantity of snow fell on them from a church roof. Rail services have all but ground to a halt across England and Wales and the emergency services . . . '

His heart sang. He could feel the happiness in his chest, somewhere just under one of his ribs, to the left. He swallowed the last of his porridge without chewing and looked at his mother triumphantly.

'That means there's no school.'

'That means you can stay at home and help your mother and father.'

'Ah, let the boy be. Kent won't be covered in snow again like this before he's an old man. Is there any bacon in the house, my love?'

His father had bent his head down beneath his mother's shoulder and she was trying to break away, grumbling. But there was a light Sam hadn't seen in her eyes before when she turned in his direction.

'Off you go then. But back by dark, mind. We're not sending out a search party for you!'

He scraped back his chair and smiled; even the porridge felt good inside him. For a moment they both looked at him from the kitchen, his father's head still bent low on her shoulder, and they all smiled. Then he went up to the attic for his sledge.

It was buried under boxes and apples and papers and a long roll of dark carpet. But there it was, intact, the sledge his grandfather had made him. He smelled it and it reminded him of a pine forest he'd once stood in – a whole pine forest.

He tried to escape then but his mother would have none of it. There were layers of horrible waterproof things he had to put on, and all of them seemed to have at least a hundred and fifty studs to button. He felt like a snowman by the time he got to the porch, and he banged the door too hard behind him, just to let his mother know how he felt.

He'd never seen snow like it in all his life. It was so amazing he had to stop completely halfway down the track, just to listen. The flakes crackled in the branches of the trees as they fell, hundreds and thousands of them. And there was no sound of the road, nothing at all. It was like years and years ago when the Romans were here, when there were no proper maps, when everything was much bigger, when the world was still undiscovered. When he reached the road it was like a white river. He almost didn't want to step on it, to spoil it – it was so beautiful. But he had to. He was going somewhere.

Two miles west, the sledge hissing at his back and thudding now and again against the back of his ankles. A robin came down once, landed on a branch not four inches from him, and looked at him with its head on one side. He found footprints crossing the road and stopped to bend to look at them. Deer – and somehow the air was still strong with their scent, with the musky dark brown of their hides. He felt he'd gone a lot further than two miles by the time he reached Wooton. It was still asleep – six cottages lying dormant under their weight of snow, for all the world like six snowballs.

His heart was going faster now, even though he didn't want it to. He was rehearsing the right words to himself, even though he didn't want to. It was the last cottage on the left, he'd known that for long enough. What if there was no-one at home? But there was a grey fur of smoke curling from the chimney. *Slow down, for pity's sake*, he told himself. *What's wrong with you?*

He swallowed hard when he got there and all at once he heard a dog, a dog squealing and yabbering and thumping behind a door. Maybe he should just go back, maybe it would all be much easier. . .

'What is it you're wanting?' A woman with light brown hair in curlers stuck her head round the door and startled him so much he nearly jumped into the neighbour's garden.

'Clare Sidbury!'

*I'm actually looking for Clare Sidbury* was what he'd wanted to say, damn it. But she vanished and he chewed his bottom lip, rattled a dry conker in the left hand pocket of his jacket. He heard muffled voices. She was most likely saying that of all people she'd hoped it might be the last was Sam Carter. . .

'Hi!'

She was looking at him and he felt so small. His mouth was dry, there weren't going to be any words. . .

'Wondered if you might like to go sledging. I just happened to be out this way, but if you've other things you have to do. . . '

'Yes! Yes, I'd love to. You'll have to wait for me, though.'

He stood outside for a moment, the door still open. He

could hear his heart thudding in his head.

'Come inside and don't take the whole lot of us to an early grave,' Clare's mother said, and he muttered an apology, thinking she might be really cross. 'Come in and get warm in the kitchen,' she went on. 'And don't worry about MacTavish, he'd as soon lick you to death as anything. Why don't you both come in later on and have some supper – it is Sam your name is, isn't it?'

He nodded and realised she wasn't angry, not really angry, not the way Mrs Henry from maths could be.

'Thank you,' he said, his voice croaky. 'That would be lovely.'

She smiled. 'All right then. You stand here and melt a minute while Clare gets ready.'

There was something funny about her voice, he thought, something he couldn't work out. He looked round the kitchen and suddenly caught sight of a collie, lying with its head on its paws and looking at him with unblinking blue eyes. There was a cuckoo clock on the far wall, clacking away loudly. He caught sight of his boots; saw there was a guilty ring of water round them. He was like a snowman.

They left in the end and the snow seemed heavier than ever. He felt so happy he thought his chest was going to burst.

'My dad says it'll snow like this for another week,' Clare said. She was wearing a bright red hat like a holly berry and under it her face was shiny and showed just and no more the dark braids of her hair. He caught the scent of her as she brushed against him and it made him feel all strange and dizzy.

'Race you to the top of the hill!' she exclaimed, and jogged his elbow.

They ended up in a heap of breathless laughter, spread-eagled under the snowflakes. When they got up they sat still for a moment, close together, looking at the patchwork pattern of the fields to the edges of the sky.

'You can see the whole of England,' she breathed, and he believed her at that moment – he was sure she must be right.

Then they got onto the sledge, Sam at the front and she behind. Her hands held round his waist and for a second, the flicker of a second, he couldn't catch his breath. Her arms were holding him.

'Ready?' he whispered at last, and he felt her head nodding behind him.

'Ready.'

They didn't go fast because the snow was too deep, but that didn't matter. It was just right; they veered off to the left through low trees and went round in a curve. A flock of birds with red wings rose up in front of them and flickered into the distance. Sam felt the breeze on his face and at last they were going straight; the sledge went over a bump and Clare's hands held tighter. He wanted this never to end; he wanted it to last for ever and ever. One last curve down to the top of the field and they got up, breathless and happy, their faces shining.

'I've never sledged before,' she said, looking right at him.

They stayed until they were too tired to climb the hill another time. They stayed until the grey skies were above them and the snow stopped falling and the wind died completely. Somewhere very far away one single star crackled and sparked like a precious stone. Sam thought that if he were to hold his breath he'd be able to hear a pin drop in Moscow.

The Ice and other stories

'Let's go home,' Clare said, and she reached out to hold his hand.

They walked like that the whole way back, until they were close to her house. The cottages shone through the trees in a sparkling of white lights. They hadn't said a word the whole way back, but it didn't matter. It had been a good silence, a silence they understood, a silence that meant more than many words.

And when they went inside the whole house was full of the scent of something, something wonderful he's never smelled before. Clare's mother must have seen the look on his face.

'Herrings in oatmeal!' she exclaimed, her eyes crinkling with merriment. 'Just the way we make them up in the north-east of Scotland!'

And Clare squeezed his hand and smiled at him, and shook her hair free. It was as though it was filled with millions of diamonds.

# The Gift

**I know what it was I wanted to tell you about, it was Christmas.** I call myself a traveller who never did, but my mother and father were both brought up on the road. It was my mother who wanted to settle, long before I was born. She'd lost my older brother to pneumonia. They'd been out in the west with the horse and cart one October, in a storm that lasted for days. Everything was drenched and frozen in the end and my brother died before they could get help for him. I think that was why they came to Dublin. I think that was it.

Well, I remember one year I was at school – I would have been six at the time. And the teacher was a Miss Munro, she was a spiteful woman. She was no taller than a pencil and the boys trembled in front of her. She should have been out breaking horses, not in a classroom breaking the spirits of children. She knew fine the names they called me and she was deaf to all of them. If she could find a way to punish me she would. I was forever going off into my own world. I'd sit there with my head on my elbow looking out into the school playground. There was one tree there, a cherry, and I loved just looking at its blossom in the spring and listening to the leaves. One morning Miss Munro must have caught me staring away at that tree and she came charging up the row, twisting my ear in her fingers until she'd hauled me onto my feet, shouting over and over –

'Are you away with the fairies, Mary Riley? Are you away with the fairies?'

It was coming near Christmas and I'd seen my father pacing again at home.

'The wolf in him wants out,' my mother whispered to me as she put a button onto a shirt. But there was the ghost of a smile on her mouth as she spoke the words, and I saw her glance at him as she spoke, though he never turned, only kept pacing.

This particular day Miss Munro had shouted at me for my shoes, the state of my shoes. I felt so small and embarrassed there in the class, and I could hear the sniggers around me. I could tell the rest of them relished my suffering. By break-time my face was smudged with crying and I felt broken in bits. And suddenly my father was there, in the corridor, and I remember he just picked me up in his arms as if I'd been a bale of hay or a young calf. It wasn't the end of the school day and Miss Munro came charging out of her classroom.

'Do you people not know what time is?' she screamed shrilly, and her red mouth seemed the only thing in her small, white face. 'Do you people have no idea what time is?'

My father laughed; I could feel his laugh as he held me, but it wasn't a bitter or an angry laugh; it was soft and just

The Ice and other stories

edged with a lace of mockery, no more than that.

'Ah, you know what clocks are, but we know what time is.'

And with that he turned and went, carrying me still in his arms, as though he was bearing me from a burning building. And all the shrieking of Miss Munro at his back was as grass blowing in the wind to him.

And out there was my father's old van, and I was puzzled, for he never came to collect me from school. I always made the journey myself, even though it was a long walk on a winter morning.

'Where are we going, dad?' I asked him as he put me into the cab, and it was warm and I caught the smell of him, from his hair perhaps.

'We're going on a journey, Moorie,' he said softly, and I know then he was in a really good mood. If he was sad he drank, and then sometimes he wouldn't speak to my mother or me for days, but just stare from the second floor window, away towards the hills, as though he wasn't there at all. But when he was happy he ruffled my hair and his brown eyes shone like river stones and he called me Moorie.

*We're going on a journey.*

And everything was in the back of his van, and my whole heart filled with excitement. I'd been off with him and my mother in the summer time, to camp by rivers and in glens, to listen to traveller stories at night by the fire. But I'd never been away in winter, when we were stuck in the city, in the fog and the freezing rain. Now we were going on a journey.

What I remember is that night. He was looking for somewhere, my father. We were nearly there, wherever *there* was. And I was in the back, lying among blankets and coats because he was afraid I'd get cold. And I remember looking out and seeing all those stars. There was a jeweller's in Dublin that had diamonds in the window set on a black velvet cloth. And that was what I thought of now as we bumped and rattled along back roads in search of the place my father wanted to find.

And some of me wanted to be there, to know what the place was, and some of me never wanted to be there at all. I wanted to stay where I was for ever, looking up at the stars as the van lurched and hummed on and on into the dark.

But at last we juddered to a halt and the silence flooded back. I had no idea what time it was and my father set up the simple tent between two trees. There was no sound in all the world and there was a frost; it was as though a giant in one of the stories of Old Ireland had breathed over everything – the trees, the fields, the hills – and turned them to a silver mist.

•

And my father taught me how to make a fire. He taught me that kindling is everything, that it's the little pieces that matter. The big bits of wood are all very well, they count later on, but there's no fire to begin with if there's no kindling. And he said it was just like that with the travellers, that the big people – the doctors and the teachers and the judges – they were all very well, but they would be nowhere without the little people, the ones who pulled the carts and cleared the fields and mended the roads.

My hands were so cold as I found pieces of wood and

The Ice and other stories

kindling and brought them to my father. But when I came back the second time he had lit the fire and was blowing on it, blowing so the flames roared, and I thought to myself that he was a kind of dragon, a magical creature that could do anything in the world he wanted.

And I crouched beside that fire and stretched out my hands to it. I felt the orange glow warm on my cheeks. And my father told me about how the travellers came to be, all that time ago in Jerusalem when Jesus was alive. For they had come looking for someone who would make the nails for Jesus' cross, and no-one would do such a thing, for he had been full of only goodness and kindness all his days. But the traveller said he would, and he lit his fire and flapped it into life with his apron. And ever since the traveller has been on the move, restless, journeying from place to place, the ghost of the nails he made shadows in every fire he makes. And I looked for the ghosts of the nails but I couldn't see them.

And I went to bed with the words still circling my head like stars, and I wondered what we were, we travellers, were we good or were we bad? Was I ashamed to be one for the sin of that first traveller, or was I glad that we were different, that we had learned to find our way in the world by different paths, by secret roads? And I dreamed that night that I was lost, and went knocking and knocking on door after door. But no-one would tell me and no-one would help me, and everyone just sent me on my way once more.

He woke me first thing next morning.

'Come on, Moorie,' he said, and I knew this was it, that now at last I was going to find out why he had brought me here.

We walked into the forest, and it was what he always called a foxy wood. It was dark; the trunks were close and branches snapped underfoot. It smelled of owls and moss and green things. But there was a path, a ribbon of a thing that wound its way between stumps and vanished in a pale thread.

'The travellers have been coming here for a thousand years, Moorie,' he whispered, and I didn't know why he whispered, but my heart fluttered like a bird in my chest and I drank in the place with all of my senses.

•

And at last we came to a glade, a round clearing in the woods, and I looked up at the branches and in them were the strangest globes. I thought at first they were hives – that was what came to me to begin with, that they were wild hives of bees. Some of them were only small and others were big as the globe of the world the headmaster had in his room back in Dublin.

'Mistletoe!' my father hissed. 'Mistletoe, Moorie! And it's been grown here by the travellers, because it has to be grafted!' And he explained to me about grafting, and about what mistletoe was. And it seemed to me it was magical, this strange thing growing in globes above my head, with its white berry that was like a river pearl, a cloudy white.

All day we picked mistletoe there in the glade. My father climbed the trees and cut little pieces and dropped them. It was my job to run here and there, collecting them from where they fell, and gather them into bundle after bundle after bundle.

And when we left in the end and drove to a nearby town

we sold mistletoe at all the houses, pieces for a few pence. It was frosty and our breath fluttered about us like scarves, and my father told me stories and taught me songs. He was so different from the way I knew him at home in the council estate among the dogs and the rubbish and the drink. Here he was different: he was himself.

And that night the rain came and a kind farmer offered us his barn to sleep in. My father wouldn't have me getting soaked; he had a horror of that after my brother's death. The barn was warm with a thick smell; we made our beds and listened to the rain on the roof above us. And the rain was like songs too. And in the night I dreamed that this was the place where Jesus had been born. I had come too in order to see this newborn king. But everyone had presents with them, the shepherds and the kings – I was just a traveller and I had nothing. But then I looked at my hand and I saw there was a sprig of mistletoe – the last one that hadn't been sold – and I went to the manger and held it above the baby's head and I kissed him.

That's what I wanted to tell you. The story of the best Christmas I've ever known.

# Kilninian

**You'll have heard the story of Caleb Ross? Oh, I imagine Caleb** had just died when I was growing up in the glen; that was a funeral they spoke about for years afterwards – people just came and came and came. He was the kindest man you could hope to meet, and somehow just *content*.

Caleb was originally from out by Nairn; he was a giant of a fellow, fine looking. He got his eye on Kilninian, that bit of ground away up on the face of the hill as you're going north, right above the manse. Often you can be coming along the road below and you'll see it covered with sun, like a gold carpet. You can see three counties from the top field above the house – it's a bonnie place all right, summer and winter.

They say he fought Donnie Grant to the last farthing for it. Donnie wasn't long for this world, he was passed it, should have moved down to be with his daughter Kitty years before. But he loved his farm and was loath to leave it.

At any rate, Caleb bought the place in December. It was a rough winter and he was snowed into Kilninian for a good three weeks. I reckon he must have lost a fair lot of livestock; when the snow comes at that height you get some almighty drifts, and though sheep'll survive a few days in it, they'll not last for ever. There were folk that said Caleb Ross had it coming; he'd robbed Donnie Grant and the Almighty was paying him back. What I do know for certain is that by February he was contemplating saying farewell to Kilninian for good. Oh, word about these things goes round like wildfire. You only need to think something in Fort William and they'll be talking about it in Inverness by breakfast.

In fact I reckon Caleb Ross had begun packing his bags. He hadn't found a buyer for Kilninian but he was damn sure he was leaving once he had. He was out by the front gate one morning, working away on one of the fences, when this fellow came by with horses. It was an old right of way that, folk had been using it since the time of Columba, especially the tinkers – sorry, the travelling people as they're known nowadays. Well, this fellow was a traveller, an old man by the name of Williamson. He'd been a pearl fisher ever since he learned to walk; he could whistle a pearl out of the Naver or the Spey like no-one alive, and he knew every bend of every river in the Highlands. He was a devout man too, Alec Williamson; he could neither read nor write so much as a word but he'd learned whole parts of the Old Testament by heart.

'This is a fine place you have,' he called to Caleb Ross that morning.

Well, Caleb looked at him like a thunderstorm, a great mallet in his hands. He'd had eight weeks of winter and not a solitary thing had gone his way since he put a foot over the threshold of Kilninian.

'Is that so?' he growled, and bent to begin hammering again. 'It may be fine to look at, but fine to live in it damn well isn't!'

Alec Williamson had crossed that pass from one glen to the other since he was a boy. Always it had seemed filled with sunlight, like walking through pure gold. He stared as if the Creator Himself would have been stung by Caleb's words.

'There's a great treasure here and don't you forget it,' Alec Williamson said, and turned away, driving the horses before him. Caleb looked up once more, turned round, the great mallet gripped in his right hand, and the words he wanted to utter seemed to melt away in his mouth. A bit of sun broke through the clouds and swept across Kilninian and the last deep drifts of snow lying against the dykes.

He thought on the traveller's words all that night and couldn't sleep for thinking of them. He'd known many a traveller with the second sight; as often as not it was death and disaster they saw coming – they were cheerful as a summer cold. Yet maybe this *bodach* really did know there was something buried on Kilninian, was telling him to look for it. There were enough stories about the Celts having had some chapel there to fill a book; in the dark of his mind's eye that night Caleb was pulling brooches out of old walls and illuminated books from buried chambers.

The following day the traveller's words were still echoing in his head like a drumbeat. For the next two weeks he hammered and mended and painted and carried; he was on his feet when the first fleck of dawn swam like a salmon into the skies, and he was still busy by the time the moon climbed like a ghost over the rowans. He was staying at Kilninian.

That May he met Elsie Stewart. She'd come over the glen to see her brother Allan who farmed at Remie (you'll remember old Donald Stewart well enough). Well, Elsie was over by chance and Caleb happened to meet her. It was her last day in the place and she'd been persuaded to go to the dance up at Milton. And Caleb had decided he'd forget about foxes and fences for one night and meet his neighbours. Once he saw her he had eyes only for Elsie. She had copper-gold hair in great bunches over her shoulders and this wide face and grey-green eyes.

She wasn't quite of this world was Elsie. When you spoke to her she looked right at you and yet you weren't sure if she was listening. She nodded but somehow you felt you'd lost her already, as though she was thinking about something else entirely. I think it was that Caleb Ross saw in her; I reckon he fell into those eyes and drowned there that night. He danced a web about her that was made of her own alluring, and she never broke free again.

They were married about half a year later, right in the middle of his second winter at Kilninian. But he carried on as though nothing had changed; he was up before dawn and out into the fields, summer and winter. Those words of Alec Williamson whispered away in his head and wouldn't be still; there was a great treasure at Kilninian and he had to find it. He ploughed up the field to the west and carried out stones that weighed half a hundredweight. When he came home for his dinner he had eyes only for the high ridge he could see through the kitchen window; maybe once it had been a temple, it was there he should search next.

Elsie Ross as she now was fetched and carried on the farm and did everything in her power to please him. But it was Caleb who seemed distant now, and the dance through which he'd spun her with a burning heart grew further and further away. But the following summer she bore him twins; little girls with her eyes and his temper – Shona and Rachel.

'Will you come in early this evening, Caleb? It's Saturday and there's nothing to be done that can't wait.'

'Is that right? Have you any idea what I still have to do before the night's out? It's as well I run this place and not you.'

He stormed out and banged the door. What was in his head was the line of the old broken wall at the very top of his ground; he'd never searched there. He dug until he hit solid rock, then stood leaning on his spade, looking down over the glen. A dragon's tongue of mist lay along its length, and here and there odd points of light shone out from it. He could name farm after farm in the twilight. Somewhere at his back the woodcocks were roding in the blue shadows, fluttering among the birches making that eerie summer call he knew so well.

And suddenly he saw Kilninian as it would be; two corn-haired girls laughing and playing in the meadow as their mother hung out clothes on the line. The light of a summer to come sweeping through and for a moment everything transformed, blessed in a shimmering of gold.

'It's a great treasure, this place,' Elsie Ross called to her daughters. 'It's a great treasure and don't you forget it!'

The vision faded and it was nightfall in late July. But the

words rang on in his head and at last he understood. He dropped the spade and began walking home, running towards the treasure that had never been buried but which his eyes had failed to see.

# The Song of a Robin

**I remember the day I left. I was seventeen and I hadn't told** them. I remember the look on my mother's face; she was cutting bread and turned round – a white oval of surprise. She cut herself and was crying, and I thought to myself: Is she crying because of what I've told her or because she cut herself?

My father was stacking wood with my brother in the yard, and they looked round at me too. I don't remember now if it was because I said something or because my mother called to them. I remember it as a kind of dream as I left the house; when I think of it I am swimming through the kind of sound-lessness there is in dreams. And their faces, my father's and my brother's, are still following me as I walk away. They have blocks of wood in their hands and they are turning all the time to follow my leaving.

It is 1914. Why am I going? Why do I leave a sleepy village at the edge of a sleepy county to join something that means nothing to me whatsoever? Is it because I am tired of going out to fetch water at dawn on white mornings when there is nothing but the cold rawness of the wind and the stink of chickens on the breath of it? Is it because I want to believe in the talk around huddled beer tables, the lure of somewhere else and somewhere new? Perhaps I am no different to the seventeen year old boy in Athens who heard the stories of warships and swords, and whose heart raced at the sound of the words. Or is that only an excuse?

I am cold and I wish they would bring me a blanket! Where is anyone in this damned place? They should be here by five thirty and it's ten past six! There's a robin there. Out on the window ledge. Wanting crumbs no doubt. Go and beg from someone else! You won't get any from me.

There was one we fed that first winter, poor fools that we were. The following winter there was next to nothing for ourselves, we would have had precious little compassion for a bird. But that winter he used to flutter down at five past eight each morning, right into our trench. I can see the faces watching now, faces of men who were to die in the long months that followed. Their faces are a strange photograph inside the book of the memory, as they watch a robin eat crumbs from the palm of a man's outstretched hand.

·

A man who is ready to take up a gun with a bayonet and rush across no man's land to kill and maim all that stands against him. And the men he is preparing to gouge and rip and blow apart have done him no more harm than that simple robin. He has no reason to hate these men, and the chances are that he will never make it far enough to see their faces.

For this is what war is about, otherwise it would not work. After that first football match on Christmas Day in 1914, the officers had to pull rank, they had to order their men back into the trenches to begin again the task they had come to complete. In case peace had broken out like Spring flowers all the way along the Western Front.

I realised all too soon my folly in running from home to this. Often enough I felt like the Prodigal Son, and yet had I gone on my hands and knees all the way to my father's house, there was nothing he could have done to save me from my fate. I had grown up on a farm and I had known small horrors: I had seen pigs whirling about long after their throats were slit, I had seen animals caught in traps – traps I had set myself. But now there was horror all about me, there was no release from it by day or night. For the few hours one managed to sleep, dreams were horrified by the cries of men who still lay undead in no man's land, hopelessly lost in a sea of mud and barbed wire and other men's blown-apart bodies.

And dream I did. Perhaps in the end we dreamed the same dream, up and down the line and on both sides of the trenches. I had been crazy about a girl called Anna in the village since I was twelve or thirteen. She had wild gold hair and eyes the colour of soft blue, eyes that always were dancing. And I dreamed one night that she came to find me, to bring me home. I was the only one awake in my dream; everyone else lay asleep all along the line, and a kind of frost covered their faces and their hands. I heard Anna's singing far away (for she was forever singing) and perhaps it was that magic which put everything else to sleep. Because goodness and

The Song of a Robin                                          137 beauty could not live in this place, it was impossible.

She stepped right down into the trench where I was and reached out her hand for mine, still singing. I stretched up into the sunlight of her face and felt the strands of her golden hair about my own. I closed my eyes for a second, knowing she had come to take me home, and when I opened them again my mouth was foul with mud, it was the middle of the night and the guns had started once more.

I remember one man saying to me – *We will never be able to see colour again*. We will never be able to see colour again. When I looked into his eyes I saw that there was nothing there, nothing left, and I felt afraid – I feared that I would be the same, that if I were to look into a mirror I would see the same blindness. But then I thought the fact that I was afraid of exactly that was proof something had survived after all! There was at least a candle flutter left that had not been extinguished.

There came a time we were on the move day and night. Of course we knew nothing, but I reckon things were bad: it must have been the winter of 1917. I was twenty years old and I felt seventy; it was as though birthday after birthday had been spent in this hell, that the years before were nothing but a dream. We were without sleep for four or five days. Once we had to take refuge in the shell of a house, knee-deep in mire, for a whole day. The ground around us shook and rumbled with explosions; the worst of it was you knew you were nothing more than a number in the most terrible game of roulette there ever had been. One man beside me went mad; he broke and fell and flailed about, sobbing uncontrollably, babbling gibberish. And the CO shot him, shot

The Ice and other stories

him in the head as though he was a dog. And he sank slowly; I remember watching him disappear into the darkness, his eyes still open, still full of unimaginable horror.

And later, when we were still there, waiting for a lull in the shelling before we began crawling out over the bare ridge once more, yard by aching yard, I thought of the madness of it. That man had survived innumerable attacks, endless nights of bombardment by the enemy, to end up shot by one of his own. And I remember wanting to laugh; I can vividly remember standing in the stench of that foul mud and water, wanting to laugh at the sheer absurdity of it all. Yet I knew that if I broke out laughing I would be shot, because once I began it would be impossible for me to stop.

But the irony is that I survived; the dice did not roll for me. I think that for a time I believed I had made it, that I was going to be all right. I had passed the great shadow and now I was into the clear. It's the way children think when they're playing some game of hide and seek; it's no different to that. There's some core of us deep inside that remains the same despite all the adult armour we wear to disguise it. I would think of it when I first woke in the half-darkness and even smile to myself: *The worst is over, it is just a question of marking time*.

Where is everyone this morning? I don't understand what on earth is going on? Someone is usually here for me long before now; I only wish I could hear what was going on anywhere else in this place! It's still strange ringing a bell, pushing a button in the wall that's soundless to me, knowing someone else will hear and come. Perhaps that's what faith is.

I suppose it was three weeks later I was sent out with the

night patrol. We were going to be moving again the following day, I'm pretty sure of that. It was so cold, so still. There was a glitter of stars but no moon. Even the muddied edge of the trench had frozen solid. We had to move so slowly, inch after inch drag ourselves over the ground in case snipers spotted us, picked us off one by one.

•

We were crossing the ridge when I was thrown backwards, my head exploding with the shell blast that ripped into the hillside. A hail of broken earth and broken men landed all around me. I landed on the bottom of the shell hole on my back, intact, except that I could hear nothing.

I was lucky they found me (at least that's what they said) and brought me back to the field hospital. They looked at me and saw a man unscathed: his fingers and toes, his limbs and his organs, his mind in one piece, almost. Was that not luck? Was that not amazing? To say you had lost your hearing sounded like a shrug of the shoulders, little more than losing a coin in the grass. I was lucky, and I was useless to them now.

So I went home and the war went on. But all the way back on trains and in stations filled with men heading the other way, streaming towards the last fading hope of breakthrough, I was locked into the silence of my own inner world. They wanted me to feel grateful because they could not see the thing I had lost, and the loss of that pearl of great price meant everything else became pale and strange and suddenly worthless. I even watched two men talking in sign language on the last train, their hands moving like rabbits in a moonlit field. I watched them until they saw me and stopped, staring at me, but I wanted to tell them, to shriek at them, that I was deaf and could not hear what they were saying.

At the end of the day it is the little things that always matter. I went back to my village; I walked down the same track I had left by all those years before, and they welcomed me – in silence. I could not hear my mother laughing as the new lamb came for its feed in the morning; I could not hear my father's axe as it thudded the wood for the stove. I could not hear the thatch of the dawn chorus, that net of song in the trees before the greyness lifted and morning began in earnest. And I could not hear Anna singing as she passed the house, the wild gold splayed about her shoulders, around the oval of her face and those blue, blue eyes.

So I left a second time. I ran away because I could not bear to hear that silence any longer, and because I could not bear to see the way Anna's eyes passed over me to the men who came home whole. At least she saw me as I was, disabled and different, bleeding inside from a wound that would never be healed again. I left one night because I could not bear to endure another morning unable to hear the singing of the birds.

Now I am old; I have everything and I have nothing. They look at me and they think, *What a miracle it was he survived those years of madness*! But they know nothing. I lie here alone in this Munich home, looking out south towards the first line of the German Alps, and I cannot hear the song of a robin as it comes in winter in hope of crumbs on a window ledge. There is no light left in my eyes.

# Clockwork

I

**Joseph Mikheil Stern was born at six twenty eight in the**
morning. His mother knew that because one of the Russian
guards who had helped them out of the Jew-hating city of
Vilnius told her the time in proud German. He was nothing
more than a young boy, with vivid orange cheeks and more
talk in him than a whole wireless. He dangled the old, worn
watch above the baby's face a few days later, just before the
convoy was broken up and scattered, and he laughed as the
baby's eyes followed it. He laughed, let out a whole river of
Russian. He made the watch into the pendulum of a great
ticking clock, flicked it back and forth above the baby's face
and laughed a great ripple of laughter as the baby's eyes and
fingers followed it, wanting. And it was because of that he
had to give the watch to the baby's mother – well, it was

because of that and also there was something about the depth of her dark eyes that held him, that haunted him, that hurt him. But she was too far away, too anxious about her baby and about where they might find sanctuary. And perhaps there was a missing father too in those deep, dark eyes.

And so began the slow journey to England, a journey that stretched out and became so slow and tortuous that it was somehow out of time. The measuring of weeks and months became pointless, the calculation of hours impossible. It was composed of events – huge events and tiny events – and all of them were weird links in a chain that led to a flight of stairs in London. And the first thing they heard as they climbed those steps together (for by that time Joseph Mikheil Stern was two years old) was the far off sound of Big Ben, tolling six slow times.

## II

My mother died when I was the same age, two years old. There came a day when I could not remember her and I cried and I cried. My father came and found me in my room; Joseph Mikheil Stern sat down by my bedside and gently pulled me round from the pillow where I lay, my eyes blind and sore with tears.

'D'you know how the sea became salty?' he asked me.

I shook my head and didn't care, but I stopped whimpering all the same.

'There was once a beautiful star that was loved and admired by all the other stars. One night she fell to earth in a great gold trail. She cried and cried because she could never have her place in the skies again, and her tears made the rivers and the lakes and the sea all salty.'

'You never have time for me,' I sobbed, my eyes blurring once more.

'Oh, yes, I do,' he murmured, and caught me up in his arms like a bear cub and took me downstairs to the workshop. He carried me among all his clocks, the clocks that he had made, and he told me their stories. And I saw them between my tears, glittering and winking, and I heard the soft whirr of their wheels, and I thought that somehow this was the very centre of the world, the place where time was made. And I wished that somehow we could gather up all the time there was and stop it, and go back and find my mother. That we could find a way into the picture of her over my bed and bring her home.

One day I woke up and listened to the whole house chiming. It was six o'clock in the morning. The air was filled with a magical polyphony of chimes and rings and tinkles. I got up and dressed the moment I opened my eyes, despite the cold of the room. My breath went in quick clouds into the air. I crept downstairs through the grey air that smelled of muslin, of bats' wings, of mothballs. I was so thin my feet didn't make the slightest sound on the steps. I watched the black and white faces of my ancestors sliding past as I walked; I saw my father in their eyes, their cheekbones, their mouths. They were all different pictures of my father.

I stopped in his workshop. The metal frames of the clocks glinted in the early morning shadows. I breathed ticking. It was like being in a room full of birds with tiny mechanical wings; shining cogs and wheels and springs fluttered whichever way I looked. All of them showed five past six.

A figure stepped forward. I was not afraid. The bald head shone a little in the early spring light; it was beaded with perspiration.

'Happy Birthday, son.'

'Thank you, dad,' I breathed. He was holding out a long gold watch. It made the room seem darker than it was; it sucked all light there to itself. It glittered like a whole river, slid through his hands and fell into my outstretched fingers, heavy as a hillside.

I dreamed that night that I climbed all the way up a great staircase to heaven, and asked God if I could give the time I had in my watch in return for my mother. But I woke up before I heard God's answer.

### III

I went up the stairs to my father's bedroom day and night. He had insisted on having the curtains drawn over every window there was, and I lost touch with dark and light. They floated into a strange twilight that smelled dank and orange. I slept when I was tired and I got up when I felt rested. Sometimes I went out by the back stairs to buy more medicine from the chemist's and I found the world glittering with rime and a gourd of moon lying still above the Cannaby Street roofs.

But my father never slept. Up there in his attic room he lay with open blue eyes, looking at the skylight. His breath dragged in and out, like sharp metal over cobblestones.

'Keep the clocks wound,' he hissed, pushing away the remains of the eggshells on his breakfast tray, the bright crumbs of yolk beside the coughed-up bits of red. 'Keep the clocks wound.'

I ran downstairs to the workshop, to the soft whisperings of the clocks. I wound them furiously, went from tiny Swiss watches to great ancient clocks twisting and clicking until my fingers felt numb and raw. But the clocks were no longer showing the same time. Some of them had rushed ahead and others had slowed, fallen into a deep sleep. They had forgotten Greenwich time and they chimed when they wanted to. There was nothing I could do to change them.

My father lay upstairs in the attic, out on the vast loneliness of his sea. The crumpled sheets were like waves, and he was drowning, all the time he was sinking a little deeper. I could not reach him; I did not know the words to call him back. All of them went dry in my mouth; they fell into grey and bitter dust. But one day, when a clock had just struck three and I did not know if it was the afternoon or the middle of the night, my lips opened. 'What is the first thing you remember?' I breathed. His eyes swivelled round in his head and he looked at me, his eyes glittered over my face. 'Blue butterflies,' he said, and the words stretched out long and magnificent. 'The world was full of blue butterflies.' And then his eyes fell away once more, could not hold onto me. 'But not any more. They've gone now.'

**IV**

London was wrapped in a muffler of fog. I was the last to leave the graveyard, even after the curate had scuttled away down Lime Row in the direction of his favourite sanctuary.

The strange thing was that I felt Joseph Mikheil Stern – my father – more alive than ever before. He was listening to the workings of the trees, adjusting a cog or two here, a spring there – and when the leaves chimed together in the October breeze he laughed, he laughed with pleasure at their harmony, their clockwork. I heard his laughter, just as I had heard it rising from the workshop below to where I lay daydreaming on my bed each Saturday morning.

I went home by back roads, streets I'd never been in before. Yet the odd thing was that the faces I saw there reminded me of people I knew. The round grin on the face of that butcher; the expression of a little jeweller peering at diamonds in the lemon-orange light of his shop. My heart began hammering. What if I were to find my father's double? What if I were to turn the next corner and end up face to face with him? The words coursed through my head, violent and shocking. I began running even before I'd properly absorbed them, dashing through back streets that were shiny with rain. I spilled someone's apples, almost fell over a puppy at the end of a lead, all but splattered my face on the stones outside St Ninian's Church. I had to keep that speed up; if I were to slow down time might return to normal, the faces become clear – and I knew then what I would see without any shadow of doubt. I had to keep them blurred, they had to be out of focus. The heavy gold of my watch kept me back, weighed me down – but I refused to slow my pace, even when my heart thundered in my chest and set my lungs on fire. I raced back up the steps to the house two at a time and stood there, breathing in great clouds of fog. The pigeons on the Cannaby Street roofs took off in a soft mauve wave.

I found my key at the bottom of my pocket. It glided round in the lock without a sound and the door slid open. I stood there on the doorstep listening to the soft electrics of the house, the comforting humming of the hall. I took my shoes off and went inside. I didn't put on any lights, despite the dimness of the house that October day. I padded noiselessly through the long turns and twists of the hall. I felt the portraits of the ancestors looking down at me, and all of them growing old. Lines dug into their faces and foreheads, their eyes sank behind failing brows. Their mouths became soft grey cries. I moved more quickly, and the thought went through my head as I went that tiny red eyes were watching me in the darkness, and I heard scuttlings on every side.

I stood in the workshop doorway, listening. But all I could hear were the clockwork clickings of the starlings, the perfect beat of the trees in the rising wind.

The Ice and other stories

# A Christmas Child

**It was a clear, frost-sharp night in the middle of November.**
Rachel had banked the fire; the thick smell of mutton soup
filled the house. Perhaps it was that that had cheered Angus;
he had had no luck with the fishing, came home dispirited
and worried after five days at sea. And because he had had no
luck, neither had anyone in the village. This was the worst
time in the year; this was the hardest of it.

On such days Angus had to break driftwood, even when
it left splinters in his hands. He needed the crisp snap of wood
from the store; it was good to come in with a bundle in his
arms and afterwards see the curl of orange flames in the grate.
Now it was peat that lay dark at the back of the fire; his eyes
dreamed in the wreaths of smoke.

There was a soft knock at the door. Who at this hour?
When he opened, he could just see the shadow of the figure
outside.

'We're going down to the point tonight, to try our luck with bringing in a ship. Will you come?'

He heard the pause between the second and third sentences. He heard his heart too, racing far harder than usual. Not only because of the lack of fish that day.

'I've told you before, Donald John, I'll have nothing to do with it. Do you and your boys not listen? I'll have no part in your business.'

The shadow moved in the doorway but did not turn away.

'Then you'll have no part in the shares either.'

Not a threat, a statement. One man left; the other closed his door. He said not a word to Rachel. They went to bed an hour later, heard nothing of the calls and deliberations out on the road at midnight. There was a soft fall of hail about one; afterwards there was not a thing to be seen or heard. The cries had been drowned; the lanterns had disappeared. There was just the endless sea, combing the rocks, boom after long boom.

The following day was beautiful. There wasn't a breath of wind. The low sun hung white in the skies and the last rowans trembled at the road end. Angus had left before first light; crept out of bed and padded down the stairs, his satchel over his left shoulder. He was going into town for this and that, though there was precious little to spend. Rachel heard the soft thud of the door, then turned and slept once more.

She was washing clothes in the house when the knock came, urgent. She called that she would come in a moment; she carried the steaming pot of water to the stone flags, sighing. She wanted the clothes to be done by the time Angus came back.

She opened the door as the figure of a girl fled. A call faded on her lips. There was a boy on the doorstep; a boy with brown eyes like hazelnuts and tight dark curls. She bent down at once beside him and she was still taller than the little soul. His eyes searched her, wide and unblinking.

'And where did you come from?' she breathed. 'Where in the world did you come from?'

It had been the best haul in many years. When Angus came back through the village they were still dividing out sacks and boxes. There was the scent of rich tobacco in the air. Robert and Cam were roaring with laughter at something; as Robert's face turned at Angus' approach the smile died on his face. It changed slowly, became at last a sourness, a sneer. The faces said nothing as he passed, yet they said everything.

He did not go in to the house then, but carried on instead to the shore. It was high tide. The vessel was out on the rocks; a small thing of dark boards and ropes, crumpled and useless. All at once he remembered a boy in school who had once taken a huge spider between his fingers and crushed it. He had smiled and looked around him, hoping the others would see, approve. Angus felt now as he had then; no different.

He went as far as he could in the direction of the wreck. The tide was fierce; he was not fool enough to venture further. And there among the dark boards he saw one single white hand. It did not even cross his mind for a moment that hand belonged to a living soul; the sea was like ice and this was mid-November. All he did was to pull away the cap from his head and close his eyes, mutter some words he would have been too shy to speak aloud in front of Rachel, and turn away to the house.

As soon as he came inside, she took his hand and led him upstairs, one finger pressed to her lips. The boy slept, more like a doll than a child, so quiet it was hard to know he breathed. She told Angus in a single flutter of words how he had come to the house.

'I understand,' he said, understanding.

Over the next weeks he seemed to do nothing but work. The days were fine – bitterly cold but beautiful. A few flakes of snow came to the island hills, made them look like the wings of a bird. The snow lay in the heather, would lie there for the whole winter.

He mended the roof of the house, his hands raw and cut with the cold. The salt from the sea was in that wind. All day he worked, until the sun went down like a ball of snow in the west.

Jacob came out to look up at him. Rachel held his hand, and the brown eyes looked up at him – both pairs of eyes looked up at him. Angus tried to think of something to say but he could think of nothing. He smiled too and it hurt to smile; even that hurt. They had called him Jacob after her grandfather.

One day he was down again at the shore and he found a sea urchin. It was no bigger than his thumbnail. He carried it home as he might have carried a fledgling fallen from the nest.

'Close your eyes, Jacob,' he whispered. He opened the little hand and laid the shell on it. 'Happy Christmas,' he said, and kissed the nut-brown smoothness of his forehead.

Later that day he knew there was something that had to be done.

'I want you to come with me,' he said to Rachel. 'I want both of you to come with me.'

They wrapped up warm against the wind and went out and closed the door behind them. It was still beautiful; the skies a winter blue, the white waves chasing in over the rocks. They went up to the village, up towards the happy laughter of the village street and a man with a squeezebox. Four of the girls were dancing; the men were laughing. They walked through the village street and the music fell away to nothing, the heads hung down, the eyes looked away. Donald John was turning back into his house. Angus carried the child in his arms; he held Rachel's hand as he walked.

He stopped and smiled and gently put the child down in front of him.

'Donald John,' he said softly, 'you gave us a share after all.'

The Ice and other stories

# The Typewriter

**My hands are on the typewriter; they are hammering the** letters I want, one after another. All this time later my hands remember. I begin slowly, like a blind man reading Braille after a long time of silence; I begin unsure and wary, as though I might be wrong, as though there may be a trap. And I hear the safe tappings, they leave their marks on the paper, and I feel a surge of joy inside, because this is the last thing I imagined.

I was imprisoned for ten months before I found myself here; ten months of silence somewhere in this great ghost of a building. I was imprisoned for telling the truth, though they said I had lied. We look from inside out, and we look from outside in.

I am a translator. I love languages, the different sounds they possess, the tiny things that alter meaning in the human voice, the letters that are silent and mutate. I love discovering the bridges that will bring a word or a whole phrase from one language to another. I can sit all night worrying about that gulf, desperately seeking a bridge, and suddenly it comes to me. I get up and hammer the typewriter with trembling hands lest I forget by the morning. We are the searchers of bridges, for all translation is a compromise.

That is what they do not understand, of course. They think in such simple terms that one word will equate another. They dream of finding a machine that will do our work for us so they are able to put in one document and have it come out like sausage meat at the other end, the same in another language.

That is why they said I lied. I was given a document to translate by the Party. It was full of lies about the past and the future, about what we have been and what we will become. It was a document to show off to our enemies. Of course I was foolish enough in what I did; I do not deny that. I changed everything that was wrong, that was not true. I made it into something beautiful from an ugly, angry declaration of hate and war. And when I sent it back to the Party I did not even do so with fear, aware that one day the knock would come on the door and the men would appear in silence to take me away. You could say I did so with the naïve joy of a child who uncups his hands and lets a butterfly go into the blue sky, its wings healed.

No, the strange thing is that their silence frightened me. A long time afterwards – months later – I lay awake and listened and wondered where they were. Because I knew I had done nothing to cover my tracks, I had gone the whole hog with my re-writing of their original. All it would take would be for one word to be found, one single word, and everything else would unravel. I saw it like a man tumbling down a staircase; landing in the end at the bottom, broken.

After that I simply waited for them. It reached a point where I almost wanted them to come, where I nearly went to them to hand myself in. It was not that I considered I had done anything wrong; I saw myself through their window and I knew.

So much so that when they did come I felt relieved. I began to cry and I imagine they interpreted my tears as grief; but if they did so they were wrong. I cried with sheer relief, because the waiting was over.

The only thing they took from the house was the typewriter; they carried it out before they took me. Even then I found it strange, almost comical, as though they might be planning to interrogate the machine, to beat and kick it until words came out of it, until it spoke or wrote, confessed the truth (their truth).

They took nothing but the typewriter and me.

•

I thought they might leave me in the padded room for ever. It was a box of silence, every wall the same. And the typewriter was not there. I longed for it as a lover longs for the beloved, and in the end the beloved becomes more beautiful and wonderful than anything else in the world, becomes in truth a kind of god. I wept and wailed for that machine because into it I had poured my thoughts and fears, my dreams and my darkest desires. I had trusted it with everything.

Now the words crawled out of the walls like caterpillars and these strange golden creatures that live in the earth, that have silken legs. They came out of the ceiling and crept this way and that, they wrote their stories in invisible ink and vanished once more. Sometimes they came in blind anger and were no more than swearwords, empty cursing, rage written in a loud graffiti to be read by my jailers. But often the words were amazing; they came as new thoughts, translations of ideas I had never understood or solved before. The words came out of the walls and entranced me; I watched them and longed to remember them on paper and could not.

•

Until today. This is where I woke up. There is one window; a long, long way above me – a narrow slit in the darkness – and when I woke up the light was just beginning. And as I lay there the typewriter came to life, woke up from the darkness. It was there, intact, and a stack of paper beside it. I got up slowly and soundlessly, as if I might frighten it, and finally I went over to it and touched it. Just as I had last seen it.

I took the index finger of my right hand and traced the whole of it, there in the silver light that poured from the window. And I remembered how I had longed to touch it in the months of the soundless room, how I had yearned for my fingers to feel the keys again.

The elation rose in me; the words welled in my head, the words that had been asleep woke up, began crowding in their thousands into my hands and I smiled for the first time in so very, very long. The light shone on the typewriter and the paper, and it shone on my smile.

I woke up in the dark with a jolt. Did I hear the crack or did I dream it? Is the dull light shining through the window sunlight or moonlight, or is it their light, their artificial light? By that they keep me confused and keep me prisoner, try to keep me afraid.

I get up soundlessly, pad over to the machine. I run my eye over it quickly, as a father might check a child for damage with the speed that is a melding of intense love and fear. Nothing. But then yes, something is gone, has been removed! The last letter, the final letter of the alphabet. While I was sleeping someone came and took it. I sit down and think of the words I cannot write, the words that are gone. So many of them are part of a childhood summer filled with light and water and laughter. Somehow now they are gone and as I type I mourn them, for the writer possesses eternity because he can always remember and recall and bring back to life what is gone. He can make things breathe anew on the page.

So they are playing a game with me, except that they know the rules and I do not.

•

In the beginning was the word. I have never understood that completely, and yet it comforted me somehow. My mother read those words as I lay under the bedclothes ready for sleep and they felt good. My mother, the warm sanctuary of my nest, and the words themselves.

But now they are dismantling the word, they are taking it away in pieces. They are watching me to see what happens; they are taking me apart as a torturer searches for the way in, for the place that will break the body and undo the mind. They are doing it slowly, because they are in no hurry and because they enjoy my pain. They are taking their revenge for what I did. They are getting their pound of flesh.

If I wait up night and day I can keep watch on the machine, make sure they can't get to it. But they will bide their time, wait in the shadows until I have to give in to my own exhaustion. Then they will come, smiling, and do what they always planned to do.

I have to write as much as I can as fast as I can, for now I have only lost one letter. They will not come for others while I sit hammering at the keys; they would not wrestle me from the machine. Surely not?

They will make me into a kind of child as they take away my letters; a child or someone damaged. I will grow smaller and smaller, my voice no louder than a bat's shriek, before I disappear, for ever.

·

So I am writing my own death sentence, my last will and testament. I think what it means to be free, out there beyond the window, in the streets above my head. If you live and laugh and ask no questions you will be all right, you will have easy days and the state will leave you in peace. But if you lift your head over the edge and look, and see things you do not understand, and begin to talk, then your door is watched. If

The Ice and other stories

you get up at three o'clock in the morning and see a slow vehicle passing through your street, and someone watching from the window, and you do not forget and make investigations, your name will be written on a list.

But it was always that way, and perhaps it always will be. It is not the engineers and the economists and the politicians they come for, the leaders of the dark regimes, it is the poets and singers. For they manipulate the heart, the others only the head, and the head can be controlled more easily by far than the heart.

But I am a translator, not a poet or a singer. For long years I slavishly obeyed, translated word for word even though I saw in front of me the lies and the half-truths. We are like rats, we human beings. We gnaw our food, we sleep in our burrows, we scurry to work. It is the small things that matter to us; we are willing to sacrifice the big things for the small. The disappearance of a neighbour does not matter as much as a slice of rich fruit cake and warm chocolate on a November night.

So we keep our heads down and we forget what we are not supposed to have seen. We tell ourselves that we will rise up in revolution when everyone else joins in, for what would we achieve alone? Except, of course, the moment never comes, and the rich fruit cake and the warm chocolate will always taste too good.

•

They have taken away the seventeenth and the twenty-fourth letters. For two days I was full of fever and could do nothing but lie on the floor in the darkness, breathing. I wandered in and out of strange dreams. They came to take away the letters and they were loud about it, like men coming to remove furniture from an old house. They were laughing all the time. Were they laughing at me or at what they were doing?

I felt the tips of my fingers where they hit the keys of the typewriter, and I thought of all the words I had hammered out. My fingertips are dark with ink. In my fever I wondered if they could take me and make me give them tracings of my fingertips to find out every word I had ever written. Are they all there at the ends of my fingers?

And then I wandered into a dream where I played Scrabble with my brother and sister, my mother and father. I saw every detail of my childhood home; I could smell the toast my mother was making for supper. And I was allowed to shuffle the letters. I had them in the lid, all the separate tiles, and I swirled them about with my fingers. And I remember what power I felt at that moment, how the others watched me as I sat there with my right hand swirling the tiles, and I said something I could not hear. I woke up and lay in the darkness between night and day, between life and death, breathing and remembering, breathing and wondering.

And I lay there remembering how I always longed for the important letters, for the letters that really counted. I needed vowels to be sure, but I grew frustrated and angry if all I had was a row of low-scoring vowels.

I wanted the big letters, the letters that mattered! And now it was the same, for they are the ones that are being taken away.

The Ice and other stories

•

It is strange to think of the first words a child speaks. How we begin. Once the river has begun, that first trickle, the flow is unstoppable. Words are everywhere, pouring out of cupboards and playrooms and garden sheds – this great heap of toys a child plays with and practises with, filling its mouth with different sounds to try and test them.

But there have been children who were kept in sheds, kept in the dark, who did not hear words and only made noises like sheep or goats. And afterwards, even when they were taken out into the light, it was somehow too late.

I wonder if enough years of solitary confinement will do the same thing? I wonder if it is possible for language to dry up in the end? Is that what will happen to me, long after the last letters have been taken away? Will I cease to think in words at all? Will even the memory of letters have gone?

As a translator I have to find the best ways to say things. I have to find ways round, to work out, to worry at new riddles until they are solved. This is no different, but it is life and death now. That is why they devised this end for me, this sentencing to death. For it would appear I can say anything I want, with this machine and this great stack of paper in front of me. Yet the converse is true. I will be able to say less and less and less.

•

The second last letter is gone. I weep because I remember a girl I loved when I was a child, and I cannot write her name, her name is gone. I think we believe children cannot love, are unable to know passionate love, and it is madness. Even though I had spoken to that girl just twice or three times, I know that I adored her. Sometimes I followed her to school. She walked with her girlfriends and I followed behind, watching every step she took. I know she knew I watched her, for once or twice she glanced round and her blue eyes shone at me. I know she loved me too. We were both twelve and in parallel classes; I watched for her when the shrill bell rang and the school disgorged its pupils like wild flocks of pigeons. It was sufficient to walk at her back and watch her shoes, her steps. I kept one turned-round glance safe as a pressed flower, precious as a cut gem. In the darkness of the room at night I saw the moment over and over and over again.

Then I did not see her. After the summer she was gone. I looked for her, desperate and frightened; at last I dared to ask a girl from her class who saw the sorrow and suffering I carried and who smirked. She told me she had changed schools, her voice cold and mocking. She turned on her heel and told her girlfriends about me in a loud voice. I felt like shattered glass. It felt as though giant hands had crushed and shattered the frame of glass I was. And now I cannot even write her name. I feel just as I did that morning when I was twelve.

•

I think it would be better if I woke up to find the whole machine had gone. It would be better than this slow torment. It is kinder to put a lobster into boiling water than into

The Ice and other stories

lukewarm water that is brought to the boil bit by bit.

What will be done with the machine in the end? (I cannot even write its name now). Will it be hung from the wall outside the prison as a warning to translators, in the same manner that men were hung from walls, mutilated? I ask with a bitter and savage mirth, because of course that will not happen. I will have been forgotten: the papers I wrote, the books I translated, the house where I lived. I will have been rubbed out, just as an eraser crosses a piece of paper and the marks of the pencil go from black to dull white and are gone for good.

And that is what we need and want, we humans. We have to be, to count, to matter! We have to be brothers and wives and sons, we have to be friends. When we become nothing and do not matter, we curl up and die. I am alive as long as I can make words, as long as I am able to write something. But I will waken up one morning with nothing left, with no more words, even the name I was given gone. Then I will be dead. I will have ceased to live.

•

I remember reading of a woman who was the last to speak her own language. She had no-one to talk to. Her people had been crushed in the onward march of change and now she was alone. All she had left was to talk to God, for God who had made her language knew her language. I believe she was saved from madness because she was still able to talk to God. That would not be possible for me.

I remember walking with my mother in a part of the urban

sprawl I hated and feared. I clutched her hand so hard it must have hurt her, though she said nothing. We went underneath a concrete bridge and the traffic roared and thundered north and south. The traffic sounded as though it was enraged. And there was a man on the concrete, the remains of a man, with his hands on backwards and with a misshapen face. He was begging, his hands clawing the air as we passed. And just at that moment there was a lull in the traffic and I heard his voice; I remember it now as if no time at all had passed. His voice was as sweet and soft as an angel's. And I looked at him as we passed, horrified and appalled and wondering all at the same time, for he possessed the most beautiful voice I had ever heard. Still I have not encountered a human voice like his.

But that was not the end. For later I remembered that voice and that man and that place and wondered what God was, that He could create such beautiful pain. For much that is blamed on God is the fault of humankind; the suffering I endure this very moment as my fingers tap was of no-one else's making. But what had that dwarf done to deserve his condition? And the voice he possessed was nothing but a curse, a cruel twist, for no-one wanted to see such ugliness in front of them. No-one could bear to look at him. And for the first time I wondered who God was that He could let this happen.

•

The letter after the tenth and two after the twentieth are gone. I fell asleep at the machine and while I slept these two were cut out and stolen. I imagine someone had to lift both arms from the machine. What if I had come to at that moment? Now I cannot write the sentence I wanted to; I am growing slower and slower – my head searches and sifts the words to find a path forwards. I am compromising all the time, just as I did as a translator. All translation is a compromise. Perhaps it is the same with an artist, a great painter or poet or composer. Somewhere outside of them is the perfect piece, the untainted masterpiece. It is for them to strain to listen, to catch each note or word or colour as fine as it can be. Each time it is closer, a little closer. But all of it is still a compromise. Now I am learning that as never before. But thus far the captors have been merciful; soon the other letters will be cut out and gone and the sentences will be useless, like an old man's steps through deep snow, slow and so sore.

When the machine is bare, its claws cut, will the torturing begin? Is this the countdown to their pleasure? When I can do nothing but scream and there is no-one to hear, when the world has forgotten who I was and no longer cares?

If I fall down this shaft into despair I will not return. There is one thing that is worse than pain and that is the fear of pain. That is the reason waiting for a prisoner to fall into despair is so delicious. Tell him the pain is coming, that it is being prepared, and he will beg and scream and roll and foam in fear. He will babble the truth and he will babble pure lies; he will babble all he can imagine and still not so much as a finger has been laid on him. That is the power of fear.

•

The Typewriter

Another of the last letters, the tenth letter, and one I cannot name at all. I am almost someone losing all that he remembers, piece by piece. Nine letters gone. There is another thing here, in addition to the light, that light's thin edge. There is a tap and its drip. It might be time, the drops and drips that are time. I chisel each sentence and am sure, so sure, to be correct. I remember coming home, seeing mother in the door, her arms open and her hair gold. I ran and ran, heart hammering, until she closed her arms about me. Is it bigger and better to dream, to see all that's coming and dream and close one's lids in anticipation, or to be there? I am not sure.

Did I do a terrible thing to be here? I do not believe so. I'm sure I'd do the same thing again. I am still translating, translating thoughts and doubts as a spider selects threads and still gets through. As long as this paper can be read and understood, I am not dead.

·

I am so alone here. More letters gone. I am not able to tell their names. This great silent nothingness. I am old. I am not ridden with angst all the same. It is almost done. I am not alone. Someone sees me in the room, is nearer and nearer all the time. Thirteen letters. God is the silence in the room. He listens. I am almost done. I am a translator in the silence. I listen and translate. I sleep little, listen instead as the men steal in, a little nearer all the time. Steal in to steal. Am I mad? I am still listening, so I am sane. I am a ghost, a moth, hiding here and listening. Most moments I am strong. Most moments I do not hate. I hope instead; I hope to see a light, a light and a door. Is it morning or night? I do not see. All I do is listen, a mole in the earth.

Almost all is stone. This is Hell. I am so alone. This hostile stone. I am lost. All I am is a name. Still I am a name.

I am.

◯◯

# Other Short Stories
## from Argyll Publishing

## An Allergic Reaction
## to National Anthems
## and other stories
## Donal McLaughlin

ISBN 978 1 906134 39 6   £7.99 paperback

'the great strength of these pieces
is their collective impact'
**Colum McCann**

'a fresh and convincing voice'
**Ron Butlin, Sunday Herald**

'issues of identity and belonging and the condition of
exile are constantly simmering'
**Scottish Review of Books**


## Selected Stories
## Brian McCabe

ISBN 1 902831 62 6   £9.99 paperback

'a writer whose craft is polished
to the point of invisibility'
**The Scotsman**

'direct, economic and masterly'
**New Statesman**

'reveals the ambition which hallmarks
Scottish fiction at its best'
**The Independent**

**Tobermory Days
– stories from an island
Lorn Macintyre**

ISBN 1 902831 56 X   £7.99 paperback

'vivid and graceful. . .

an excellent short story collection'

**The Herald**

'vibrant and vivid'

**Sunday Herald**

'beautifully realised. . . compelling'

**West Highland Free Press**


**also the sequel. . .**

**Tobermory Tales
Lorn Macintyre**

ISBN 978 1 906134 78 7   £7.99 paperback

---

Available in bookshops or direct from Argyll Publishing,
Glendaruel, Argyll PA22 3AE Scotland
For credit card, full stock list and other enquiries
tel 01369 820229  info@argyllpublishing.co.uk
or visit our website www.argyllpublishing.com